GINOLA:
From St Tropez to St James'

David Ginola

HEADLINE

First published in 1996
by HEADLINE BOOK PUBLISHING

10 9 8 7 6 5 4 3 2

British Library Cataloguing in Publication Data

Ginola, David
    Ginola: from St. Tropez to St. James'
    1.Ginola, David 2.Soccer players - France - Biography
    3.Soccer players - England - Newcastle - Biography
    I.Title
    796.3'34'092

ISBN 0 7472 1799 8

Typeset by
Letterpart Limited, Reigate, Surrey

Printed and bound in England by
Mackays of Chatham PLC, Chatham, Kent

HEADLINE BOOK PUBLISHING
A division of Hodder Headline PLC
338 Euston Road
London NW1 3BH

GINOLA:
From St Tropez to St James'

CONTENTS

Acknowledgements   ix

Introduction – *L'Attraction des Opposés* –
        Opposites Attract   1

Chapter One – *Chez Moi* – Home   5

Chapter Two – *Les Rêves* – Dreams   13

Chapter Three – *Le Débutant* – Debutant   25

Chapter Four – *La Réalité Mord* – Reality Bites   31

Chapter Five – *La Passion* – Passion   41

Chapter Six – *Les Vedettes* – Stars   51

Chapter Seven – *Le Crime* – Crime   61

Chapter Eight – *Parents et Amis* – Kith and Kin   73

Chapter Nine – *La Confrontation* – Confrontation   79

Chapter Ten – *Le Pays des Geordies* – Geordieland   89

Chapter Eleven – *Vive la Différence* –
        Long Live the Difference   99

Chapter Twelve – *Affrontement Culturel* –
        Culture Shock   107

Chapter Thirteen – *Le Grand Huit* – Rollercoaster   117

Chapter Fourteen – *Une Minute* – One Minute   133

Chapter Fifteen – *Le Naufrage* – Shipwreck   145

Chapter Sixteen – *Le Calme après l'Orage* –
        The Calm after the Storm   159

Index   175

For my boy Andrea

David Ginola collaborated with
Amy Lawrence in writing this book.

Acknowledgements

With thanks to Ian Marshall, who kept faith throughout; Olivier Godallier, who made sure everything ran smoothly; Gill Rosner, whose bilingual excellence and enthusiasm proved invaluable; and Amy's mum, Elayne Cyzer, for keeping her relatively sane.

INTRODUCTION

L'Attraction des Opposés
Opposites Attract

It takes all sorts to make a world

Proverb, anon

There's only one David Ginola? Kind of. I couldn't tell you about Jekyll and Hyde, but I am one person who enjoys two very different lives. The contrast is as stark as the black and white stripes on my chest.

My name is David Ginola. I play football for Newcastle United in the North East of England. Come with me into the dressing room at Anfield. The air is thick with the smell of camphor oil, the sound is a haze of studs and wisecracks and rallying cries. In the distance, we can hear the crowd outside setting a feverish tone for this momentous match, Liverpool v Newcastle. We feel the adrenaline pumping and hype each other up to be ready for 90 minutes of burning pressure and intense action. We must win.

Je m'appelle David Ginola. I was born just outside St

Tropez in the South of France. Come with me to the beach. The sand is soft and the sea flickers between blue and green. The sun sets the tone for the way of life, warm and open and friendly, occasionally punctuated by the mistrals, a refreshing wind which blows from the mountains towards the Mediterranean. It's quiet, *tranquille*. We love to have a siesta, a quiet time to enjoy the sun, the seagulls in the air, have a good lunch, spending about three hours at the table with friends and family. Very relaxed, no troubles. If I need to unwind, it is the perfect place. It's my oasis of calm.

Anfield is a vibrant cauldron of noise. The Toon Army stand in a mass behind one goal, urging us towards victory. This is football as theatre, and the drama, nerves and excitement roll around the stadium. With only one minute gone, disaster! It is the Liverpool fans who rise to herald the first strike. This game is an emotional rollercoaster. Les Ferdinand scoops in a brilliant equaliser on the turn, and, within minutes, I grasp the ball and summon all the fire in my soul to lash the ball into the net. We are winning 2–1. My Newcastle team-mates rush round me and we are elated.

La plage, the beach, not far from my house, is the focal point for all my friends and family. People pop in and out throughout the day, have a drink, maybe something to eat, and conversation and laughter flow freely. A friend of mine just stopped by for a minute and left his car running. The engine ticked over until he left an hour later. That's the life here. There is a song special to this region which epitomises the attitude: 'There is a tree and on the tree there is a branch, and it might fall on my head so I have to cut it off. But not today, maybe tomorrow.' It's a beautiful, meandering tune. We always put off what we have to do now for some time in the future. Procrastination is a way of life in the South of France. Urgency is not a concept we understand.

The game swings ferociously this way and that. We are momentarily deflated as Liverpool's pacy football yields another goal. 2–2. We sweep down to the other end. Attack attack attack! We must win. The Colombian Tino Asprilla crafts another goal for Newcastle, a sensational curler which leaves David James stranded. We are ahead again, 3–2. Come on United! The minutes tick by. Goalmouth chances flash past like shooting stars. Some 40,000 hearts are in their mouths. Liverpool score again, it's 3–3. Come on Newcastle, we must win! We are chasing the ultimate prize. Don't stop running, don't pause for breath! Sheer noise is crackling from four sides. The 90 minutes are up; it's injury time. Stan Collymore strikes from an acute angle . . . We lose 4–3. My mind is jangling.

CHAPTER ONE

Chez Moi
Home

My sweet life ain't nothing but a thrill
I live the life I love and I love the life I live

Muddy Waters

My first memory of football is firmly imprinted in my mind and in my nose. My father René was an amateur player with our local team, Association Sportive Maximoise (ASM), and every Sunday afternoon my mother and I would go to watch my father play. It was a treat to go into the ASM dressing room with my father. I was instantly intrigued by the heady smell of the camphor oil they rubbed on their legs. It's a very special smell. I sat in the dressing room near my father; I watched him put the oil on his legs and I was intoxicated by the aroma. I hankered after it, telling myself: 'One day, I want to have this oil on my legs as well.' I didn't have to wait too long for my first football dream to be fulfilled. After a match in the regional championships, I asked my father to put some oil on my legs and he obliged. I felt like a real footballer. The smell meant everything. It's better than jasmine, or perfume, better than anything.

My father played for ASM until he was 38 years old. He was a right back, and if we played together he would have had to defend against me! As soon as I was old enough to leave the house I was at the football ground, the Stade Gerard Rossi. The pitch at the stadium was bereft of grass; there were tiny stands, a cramped dressing room and a little bar selling crisps for the crowd. But when I was a boy it looked huge. I used to ride there on my bicycle to go to support my father.

Welcome to Sainte Maxime. This is the village where I grew up, beside the sea in Provence, a region in the South of France that sprawls along the Cote D'Azur. The blue coast. My St Maxime, full of charm, sits on the edge of a bay, with St Tropez directly opposite on the other side. The sea lies in between, and a boat sails across to connect the two neighbours. According to local legend, the two saints lived together on this stretch of coastline, until one day they had a terrible argument and Tropez went to live on one side of the bay so he could be away from Maxime, and Maxime stayed here, so he wouldn't have to see Tropez. They never spoke to each other again.

The area assumes a completely different character as the seasons change. In the winter it is beautiful, peaceful, unspoilt. The population consists mainly of fishermen and placid weekend visitors. In summer it's completely transformed, overwhelmed by vibrant colour, vivid lights and vivacious crowds. St Tropez's winter population of 10,000 is boosted to 90,000, which makes an enormous difference to the ambience. The place revolves around having a really good time. The atmosphere is brilliant, because it's all for life. No pressure, no problems. It's infamous for summer parties, some of the best known in the world. We can barely recognise our town because there are so many people, so many foreigners. But like every party, there is a mess to be cleared away afterwards and if the tourists make our village ugly or dirty, they trot nonchalantly back to their cities without caring about what a state they have left in St Maxime. All the locals agree that winter is infinitely better. Everyone wants the holidays to end so we can return to the clean, peaceful town that we love. The air is pure, the sea is clear. We can relax.

Growing up in the 1970s, St Tropez and St Maxime were like two separate universes even though they are only a stone's throw apart. In the former lived the enigmatic Brigitte Bardot; it was a scene of hip nighttime gatherings and glamorous girls with long legs and false eyelashes. In the latter, lived David Ginola; it was a scene of cooking with my mother and playing football with my father. Although I was born in Gassin, in the hills on the out-skirts of St Tropez, I spent my childhood in the calm of St Maxime. As far as I was concerned, my exotic neighbours in St Tropez lived in a mythical world. I could have gone to spy on Brigitte through a hole in the fence, but it didn't cross my mind. When I went to see my grandparents in St Tropez, I hardly came into contact with the high life. I didn't care about the jet-set and their lifestyle. Of course I know it well now. I like the bright lights, but only up to a point. It's important not to get blinded. A footballer I knew of called José Touré lived in St Tropez. He had so much natural talent, but he got caught up in a whirl of alcohol and cocaine and lost everything. He had it all and rather than nurturing it, he destroyed it. It's a fine line.

I was passionate about football from a very early age. I relished the taste of it from the start. From about two years old, as soon as I could walk, I was kicking a ball about. I have a very vivid memory that I loved football as soon as I could work out how this plastic round thing could move. I think I was born to play football.

My father introduced me to the game. One day, he just kicked me a football, we played together and he asked me what I thought. I replied, 'Yeah, I like it,' so we played again. And again . . . I have fond memories of us practising, although once I got used to playing with my friends I didn't want to play so much football with my father any more. He never pushed me; he was happy to let me develop at my own rate.

He always said, 'My son will do what he wants to do in his life,' even though he was desperate for me to become a professional player. Maybe in a way he was living his own aspirations through me. He always wanted to be a professional himself, but it was a fanciful wish because he had no option but to work hard. When he was growing up in the late 1940s, just after the war, life was just too difficult to think about making a living as a football player. If he had told my grandmother, 'I want to become a football player,' she would have said, 'No chance. You don't live in a big city and you have to work because money is too important.' It was the wrong era for people who dream because, at that time, it was unrealistic to think beyond the next few francs.

When I was first offered a professional contract, he couldn't believe it. It was as much a dream for him as it was for me, and now he is so proud. At the very beginning, he did so much for me, he made everything happen. He gave me the solid foundation to enable me to do what I do today. He was a great influence. He gave me the hunger for football.

After all those years when I used to stand by the touchline and watch him, the roles were reversed and my father always came to watch me play, every weekend. He said the usual things that a father says to a son. He was always very positive, but he made sure I kept my feet on the ground. 'Don't lose sight of what's important in life,' he

8

said. Wise words indeed! Football can seduce you into following the route to success, then it can smash you off the road. I have reached some incredible highs thanks to football, but it has pushed me close to the depths as well.

I played every evening in the street outside my house with my friends. In the summer, when there was no championship, we would be knocking the ball about for hours, until the sky darkened at about 10 o'clock at night. The game was interrupted only if a car came by and we all rushed to the side of the road until it passed. Sometimes we played against a nearby wall, marking out goals and inventing rules; or else, not far from my house there was a patch of ground near a river surrounded by bamboo. It was an ideal pitch for us; we scratched out goals in the ground and played in our own little stadium. I still see kids with footballs in all the same places now.

For me, playing football is all about the competition, not the training. There is nothing wrong with a kickabout in the street, and I'm sure it was good for me, but I prefer to have an edge, some rules, a referee. I want to win; I want competitiveness all the time. If I play any sort of game with anyone, I have to win. I can't stand losing. If I play tennis, golf, even a game of cards, I need to win. I can't play just for fun. It must be a pain in the neck for my friends. They might be very relaxed, saying, 'Hey, come on David, let's have a good time.' No way! Not for me. If you just want to have fun, you have to play with someone else! But I think it's a good thing that I'm a bad loser.

My father always said that was the difference between me and my younger brother Sebastian. I always knew what I wanted to become and my approach was absolutely ardent. My mother and father didn't have to push me because I did it all by myself. I didn't need to be urged all the time, but with my brother it was always 'Come on

9

Sebastian. You have to do this.' And he would sigh and go, 'OK.'

He had ability too, and the same opportunities as me. He played centre back and had many of the right qualities, but mentally he didn't want it. My father remembers telling Sebastian: 'If there is no game, it isn't a problem for you. You go and play around with your friends. But for David, it's everything to him. He can't imagine missing a game.' That was the difference, a question of passion. My brother lives in my shadow all the time. Probably the only problem I have in my life now is that I don't really know him. I think it stems from the fact that I left home too early. I was 13 years old and my brother was nine. We were both quite young to live separately from each other. It was a period where it's very important that you are together, to understand who you are. I missed this period a lot; I missed my brother. It took a long time for us to catch up with one another. There comes a moment when you wake up and realise what is important in life. Now we are close. We found each other last summer when we spent a lot of good time together during the holiday after my first season with Newcastle. We made up for lost time.

As far back as I can remember I used tricks when I played. It was something that came naturally, rather than being the result of hours spent practising skills. When I played in another village against the local clubs, people would whisper, 'Oh, that is David Ginola.' At seven years old I was strutting around! My parents have some film at home on super eight; it's very precious to the Ginola family. I watch it from time to time. I was so quick and so easy with the ball compared to my friends. As soon as we had organised games, I played in the centre of midfield, involved in the heart of the game. I was the captain of my team from that age.

I always played with bigger boys. All my neighbours

10

were older and taller than me. They used to get very angry because I would beat them with the ball – a touch here, a dribble there – and I was so much younger, perhaps five years their junior. But they couldn't clatter into me because my father would be on the touchline watching eagle-eyed. If anyone dared to go in a little too firm for comfort, he would yell at them, 'Come on, play fair! Behave yourself.' I have always taken a lot of tackles, but I am lucky – I have never been badly injured throughout my career. Touch wood.

I didn't want to make a big deal of it, but I was better than the other kids. All the people in the area claimed that I had to play football. It was all I wanted to do. There was nothing else for me as soon as I realised what it is to play with the ball. Then, when I found out there is a job you can do with this ball, I thought, 'I must have this.' I needed it. Inside myself I knew it was really important to me. I couldn't live my life without it.

I used to babble to my friends all the time, saying, 'I'm going to be a footballer.' They replied, 'Oh piss off!' But they didn't understand my passion. We had a game on Saturday afternoons and even at seven years old, I had my routine. I preened in my kit, cleaned my little boots, folded my towel and prepared my bag. I waited in the kitchen and focused on the game ahead. I sat on the table, concentrating, staring straight ahead, miles away. If I looked out the window and saw the weather was no good, my stomach would churn. Then my father would come in and say, 'David, no game today.' I bawled 'No game?' then ran into my room and stayed there, crying all afternoon. I had waited for the game all week long. At school I was interested only in waiting for Saturday.

CHAPTER TWO

Les Rêves
Dreams

The streets were full of footballs

Samuel Pepys

I am not a kid from the street. My home life was quite normal. With my mother and father there was always something to do. I didn't need anything more. I had everything I wanted. My parents are good people, lovely people. My father's family are from Genoa in Italy and, although my mother is French, where she hails from is right on the Italian border and there is a very strong Italian influence. My parents worked from when they were very young. My father made torpedoes for submarines in a factory in St Tropez, while my mother worked for France Telecom. They retired together when they reached 60 years old and now they put all their energy into having a good time, a just reward because they laboured long and hard all their life to make a happy family. That means everything to me. I really have to thank my parents for who I am now.

My mother, Myrielle, and I are very much alike. We didn't always click because we have the same character. I shout, she shouts. Every Sunday we would spend from 9.30 in the morning until one o'clock in the kitchen. It was a weekly ritual. We often cooked pasta – but not pasta from the packet – real, fresh pasta, and maybe a cake. I learned how to cook and now, with my family, I do the same. My son has his hands in the flour and we bake together. It's very important to me and it stems from my family's Italian origins. In Italy everything revolves around *la mamma, la pasta* and *i bambini*. It's the foundation of their whole culture.

I had a very ordinary family childhood. Nothing spectacular. At school I was neither excellent nor stupid, I was a middle-of-the-road schoolkid. I always passed my classes without a problem, but in truth I was never that interested. When I was in the classroom I felt claustrophobic. I stared through the window, longing to be outside in the fresh air. I wanted to run a lot, to play football. To me, youth means being outside with all your friends. I was terrible in the classroom; it was a massive problem for me to stay inside for one or two hours. I couldn't concentrate. But I suppose you have to.

Only one thing has stayed with me from my schooldays, an essay I composed about my future when I was nine years old. Our assignment was to write an essay about what we wanted to do when we grew up. I scrawled pages and pages about my wish to become a professional footballer. This is the first page of my essay: 'Above all I would like to be a footballer, to be a professional in a big team like St Etienne. I really like sport. I would like to be in the stadium with my friends, to get ready for big matches, with our coach who tells us how to win against the other team. I'd like to finish first in the championships. With the money I would earn in this job I could buy a nice house for my parents and then I could be a coach myself.' Simple really. My mother still keeps the essay at home in France. Hopefully, it's a reasonable example for all children who have a dream. Aged nine I wrote this essay, and then years later I signed a professional contract and the dream became reality.

I learned English at school for seven years. I also did six years of German, but that must rest in a redundant part of my brain because I don't remember anything. I thought German was boring and I had no interest. But I was brilliant at English, thanks to one special reason: not some sort of premonition that I would one day play in England but because I fell in innocent love with my teacher, Madame Bonnemain. I sat at the front bench and I stared at her, wide-eyed, constantly. I focused so hard on everything she said. Every time she asked a question I threw my hand up. She couldn't even finish the question. Me, me! I can answer. Pick me! One day she visited my parents to explain the sorry tale to my mother: 'I can't teach in David's class because he looks at me so intensely, I can't teach. I told him not to look at me like this. I can't speak because I know that he is watching me with this obsessed expression all the time.' I was 11 years old.

My life was completely dominated by sports. As far back as I can remember we went skiing every winter in the mountains, and I enjoyed sailing and tennis in the summer. I played sport of some description every day after school. In France, there is no school on Wednesdays, so in the morning I had tennis, and football in the afternoon. On Saturday I was obsessed with the game ahead from the moment I woke up. Sunday was family day, a time to be at home, helping my mother to prepare our leisurely lunchtime meal before an afternoon at the Stade Gerard Rossi.

To head for the snow-capped Alps each winter and spend

the summer hopping on and off boats might sound very privileged, but you don't have to be some kind of special star to live this pleasant existence down in the South of France. People in England might think you have to be posh to spend your time on the beach and the slopes, but it's very much the way of life on the Cote D'Azur. They are classless recreations in France. Anyone can live like that. It's not considered an extravagant lifestyle, it's as common as going to the pub in England. The English think that if you live in the sun it must cost you a fortune, but that idea is associated with jet-setting or holidays, which means spending money. Make no mistake, it's not free, especially in the summer when the prices go up to greet the tourists. But everyone can get to the mountains or spend some time on the beach and the air you breathe doesn't cost a centime. It's all to do with quality of life.

I never had football heroes. There were no big posters in my room, and I never pretended to be Platini or Giresse or Tigana. That's not my personality. My heroes when I was small came from comics not centre midfield – Ironman, Spiderman and Daredevil. I was a skinny kid and I looked at Ironman in amazement. I was so impressed with his red and yellow costume and his protruding stomach and chest muscles. I used to try to draw pictures of all his muscles at school. Now, my only hero is my son, Andrea. It's in his eyes. He has something so natural, so naive, which to me is really important. It's so hard to find someone today who is very honest, very pure in his mind. When my boy says 'Daddy I love you', I know it's true. I know it's real. It's not like someone who comes up in the street and says 'I love you'. Maybe when they go behind me they'll put a knife in my back.

I didn't watch much football other than locally in St Maxime. I just wanted to play. But the 1984 European Championships made an impression on me, like every boy in France. When I watched the final, I sat right up close in front of the television screen – it was a brilliant team and a brilliant result. Michel Platini, who was the inspiration as France sailed to the final, scored from a curling free-kick to set us on our way to a 2–0 victory over Spain in the Parc des Princes. It was a fantastic boost for the country. My mind was made up: I wanted to play for France! I could only dream that I would one day play in that famous stadium in the blue shirt of my country. I always wanted to play for teams I saw on the TV. I remember the classic European Cup tie in 1977, when St Etienne played against Liverpool, who had a certain Kevin Keegan in their side. That was when I wrote my essay and I was convinced St Etienne were the team for me. They beat a vintage Liverpool team 1–0 in France before going down 3–1 at Anfield. The football throughout the tie was beautiful. Little did I realise that one of the Liverpool goal-scorers that day would have such an impact on my life almost 20 years later.

When I was 11 years old, I entered a tournament with a team from St Raphaël, a nearby town. It was an international tournament including sides like AC Milan. As I was registered for St Maxime, I couldn't officially represent St Raphaël, but I really wanted to play in the competition so I played with a false licence, under the alias of Eric Boyer. We won the event and as the whole team was lining up to collect our winners' medals I was at the back, trying to keep a low profile. The man at the microphone announced, 'And the winner for the player of the tournament award is . . . Eric Boyer!' I was just mucking around with the other boys, so did not hear. 'Eric Boyer from St Raphaël,' boomed the speakers. I thought, Oh God, that's me. I went to collect the medal and the man enquired, 'Eric, how are you?' Eric was fine, I can tell you.

A man from the AC Milan squad was so impressed he

asked for my address. The next day he arrived on our doorstep to talk to Eric Boyer's father about the possibility of signing me up. My dad was very flattered, even if he was slightly thrown by the situation. He got out of it by explaining I was too young to go to Italy. What a career Eric might have had in Serie A, but it wasn't to be.

My footballing rise developed apace and I didn't have to wait long before another club representative courted my father. Each year there is a regional selection, and a scout from Nice came to watch me play. I was aware he was on the touchline. He liked what he saw and came later to our house to ask the Ginola family if Nice could sign me for their *centre de formation*, a kind of football school. He had a long discussion with my father, repeating that he wanted to have me at the club. It was a professional club! It was in France and not too far away! I was terribly excited. My father was obviously interested, but he was also concerned that it would interfere with my education. Aged 13 there is never a guarantee a boy is going to make the grade, as I would later discover. The scout explained that I would still attend a normal school, but would be coached at the club in the evenings and play for them on weekends. I had an important decision to make as at the same time I was also invited to join a ski school. Much as I loved skiing, it was always second choice.

I was crouching behind the door, listening to everything. The more questions I overheard my parents ask this guy, the more I gulped, 'This is never going to happen.' I was very young to leave home, for my parents and my brother as well as for myself. I came into the room and begged them to let me try. My father looked me straight in the eyes, and he could sense how important it was to me to take the opportunity. 'I can't say no. OK. Go!' He confirmed my choice.

Nice is only about an hour away from St Maxime. Every

weekend my parents came to visit, and if I had a problem, they could easily come and see me. It wasn't as if I was spending months away from them, but we were a very close-knit family, and when you have to leave everything, it can be very hard. At first I thought, 'Yeah I want to go, I'll have no problem being away.' But I was only 13 years old and I couldn't really know what I wanted. At that age you don't have the experience to make a good judgement on life, you don't know how to make an important decision. You can think something one moment and regret it afterwards. Maybe it was a bad choice, because I wasn't mature enough for it. In fact, once I had spent some time in Nice I realised my family life was so important to me. While I was away, lying on a bed in an unfamiliar room, I would wonder about my mother and father and Sebastian.

Aged 29, I realise that if I could do it all again I would make another choice. I would definitely have tried, but I would have gone later, maybe after a couple more years in St Maxime. I was a kid, not really an adult yet in body or mind. With the benefit of hindsight, it was too big a decision for a kid. I was incredibly naive.

It was time to fend for myself. Most of my new friends in Nice were more mature than me. There is a big difference between growing up in the city and in a village. When I arrived in Nice I felt like one of those cinema characters from Smalltown, USA, who wanders goggle-eyed around the New York metropolis. If I have something to say to parents now who want to put their children in a football apprenticeship, I would say wait until you are sure they are adult enough to cope. The one positive thing to come out of it was that it made me stronger and I needed to harden up because I was too innocent. I hadn't experienced any confrontation before and I suppose I needed it to become more mature.

My new life was a disappointment to me every day. I was quite miserable. It wasn't really football and it wasn't really school. The system was similar to a boarding school in England. I had a normal day of school, I went to training in the evening, then there was a coach to take us back to school, where I did my homework. I slept at the school, had breakfast at school, and it started all over again . . . Nice was boring. It was a regimented existence. It was the worst time of my life.

As well as being the new boy from out in the sticks, I was very small and thin, which hardly helped. Sometimes I was so frustrated I wanted to fight with someone but I was so little. People can't believe that when they see me now. With a half-mocking, half-dubious expression they say they cannot believe I was ever thin. But it's true. Ask my parents! My body developed naturally at 17. But even then I was still thin and had to go to the gym to do a bit of body-building. I gradually became stronger. I wouldn't mind seeing some of those guys from school now to see if they still want to act the big-shot bully.

I was permanently in trouble and it was so hard for me to wake up every morning knowing I was going to have another bad day. There was nothing but confrontation with someone all the time, because every day is a fight when you live with a lot of children: about clothes, about a girlfriend, about a haircut. Anything. I was mystified by everything that was going on around me. It wasn't like this in my home, in my town. Everyone at Nice was angry or sad or superior all the time. There were some good guys as well, but unfortunately not enough of them.

It was during my stay in Nice that I discovered the fairer sex. I was always popular with women, but at first I couldn't have been less interested. My interest was football. That was all I cared about – football, skiing, my mates, playing in the woods. I was a late developer. I always attracted a lot of attention, but it wasn't a concept that attracted me at all. When I was younger all these women used to say, 'Oh he's so gorgeous, he's so cute, if only he wasn't so young! It's not worth it, he can't get it up yet!'

When I went to Nice, I started to open my eyes, because when you arrive in high school, when you're a boarder surrounded by other boys, you sit around and talk and inevitably you look around at whatever everyone else is looking at. They all talked about women. 'Have you seen this one, that one, she's not bad . . .' I was there and I looked too. I thought. 'Hmmm, they're not wrong. There might be something in this. I think I could be onto a good thing here.'

I looked into it a little closer, but at the beginning it was quite difficult for me because I simply wasn't used to it. And the first time that your heart starts beating at 100 miles per hour you ask yourself what the hell is going on? I felt out of control. This isn't anything like walking onto a football pitch! This is all about touching and kissing – this is a different world.

Over the weekend I either stayed at the *centre de formation* if I had a match, or if there was no game I went home to St Maxime. So it was when I was at school during the week that all the boys and girls hung around. I had girlfriends, most of whom I have never seen since. There were two girls who were both called Isabelle; they were older than me, and they were very interesting because of that. And I can't forget the most beautiful girl in the playground who always wore green boots, in fact that's what we called her. I'll always remember this girl. Everyone wanted to kiss her. 'Green boots' was her nickname and we chatted about her for hours. There were also a lot of platonic relationships. After all, I was only 14.

Sometimes I bump into people from school again, they

come and tap me on the shoulder and say, 'Do you remember me?' and I say 'No!' The trouble is they are talking about 15 years ago and I can't possibly remember everyone, and because I am in the public eye there are more people that know who I am than I recall.

I finished my studies at 16. I wasn't a scholar; but I had a good all-round education – mathematics, physics, natural science, philosophy, and French literature, such as Charles Baudelaire, Artur Rimbaud, Alexandre Dumas and Jean-Paul Sartre. My philosophy teacher thought I was something of a poet, as when I wrote, my thoughts would spring off in every direction. When I took my exams, my text was a poem by Baudelaire called *L'Albatross*, all about the destiny of the poet. I had to explain what the author means, and analyse why he says it. I had a flair for this. I can read something and understand the context very quickly. This stood me in good stead for my life in professional football. It's important to be sharp and to grasp the nuances in an existence which moves at great speed.

I think what I learned was important. Now I can have a conversation with anyone about anything. I am interested in historical stories and movies about things that happened in the past, like *Schindler's List*, *The Mission* and *JFK*. Everybody now should know the story of their country, the wars and the problems it has faced. I think it's a crucial part of life. I can't believe that some children in France don't know the history of the nation.

I also enjoy gangster films like *Scarface*, with Al Pacino, and anything with Robert de Niro, and French films starring Gerard Depardieu. If I had needed to carry on my studies, I was all set to take law. I liked the idea of helping people to achieve justice and I wouldn't have objected to sporting a suit to go to the office every day!

Once I had passed my exams, Nice didn't want me

Two lifelong passions: the sea and football.

The Association Sportive Maximoise mascot. Papa Ginola looks on, middle of the top row.

The young captain goes for glory.

At school, writing about his dream: the life of a professional footballer.

Ginola
David

Samedi 22 Mai

Rédaction

Plus tard, j'aimerais par-dessus tout faire du foot = être professionnel dans une grande équipe comme celle de St Etienne. Le sport me plaît beaucoup, j'aimerais me retrouver sur le stade avec les copains, Préparer des grands matchs avec notre entraîneur qui nous donne des conseils pour gagner nos adversaires et finir premier du championnat. Avec les sous l'argent que je gagnerais en faisant ce métier je pourrais acheter une jolie maison pour mes parents. Ensuite je pourrais faire entraîneur d'une équipe. Ce n'e

TSVP

It's official! Papers from Toulon for 19-year-old David.

| 1986-87 | FÉDÉRATION FRANÇAISE DE FOOTBALL
Ligue Nationale de Football
24, Boul. de Courcelles, PARIS-17 | N° 4322 |

JOUEUR ~~PROFESSIONNEL~~ ou STAGIAIRE
SPORTING CLUB DE TOULON ET DU VAR

NOM et Prénom __GINOLA DAVID__

Né le __25/1/1967__ à __GASSIN__

Nationalité __FRANCAISE__

Domicile __Che. Buges-Les espirides-BAT C 1__
__83110__ __SANARY__

L'Administrateur de la L.N.F.   Le Secrétaire du Club,   Le Titulaire,

Carte rigoureusement personnelle, valable seulement pour le Championnat Professionnel

VOIR AU VERSO

Aiming for the big time at Matra – winning against mighty Marseille in the 1990 French Cup semi-final. (*Presse Sports/Action Images*)

A proud Matra Racing team lines up for the final in 1990. Ginola is on the front row, second from the right. (*Sipa/Colorsport*)

National team debut against Albania in Tirana, November 1990. (*Presse Sports/Action Images*)

King of the Parc des Princes, home of PSG. (*Sipa/Colorsport*)

Always a battle against Marseille, the club of the South.
(*Presse Sports/Action Images*)

(Above) Good times for PSG. Winning the French Cup in 1993 and (below) thrashing Real Madrid 4–1 in Europe. (*Presse Sports/Action Images* and *Sipa/Colorsport*)

A couple of years later and Barcelona are on the receiving end.
(*Clive Mason/Allsport*)

any more. I was too frail and they weren't prepared to take the gamble that I might fill out. When I finished school, my father came up to the club and asked the chairman of Nice, 'Do you want to sign David on an apprentice contract?' They were very frank: 'No, and the reason is because David is too thin. We don't see him becoming a professional in the next three years.' Even though I wasn't exactly fond of Nice, I felt gutted to be rejected.

I think I am an honest guy and if I was coaching kids I'm sure I would take my time in making a final decision on someone. I would try to be responsible to everyone's feelings, to be a little more patient. At Nice they tried to teach me everything too quickly. You aren't developed enough at 13 or 14 to give of your best as your body isn't fully formed. At 14 years old you're clearly not the finished article. As you develop your skills, you have to grow up physically as well as increasing your ability. I had legs like sticks, *jambes des baguettes* as they were described, and people didn't take time with me. It's very important to wait with children.

At first I thought my career in football was over before it had even begun. It was a hell of a knockback. My father called a friend of his who worked with the team at Toulon. He said: 'David is finished with Nice, do you want to look at him?' I had a trial, and the youth manager Gaby Robert drooled, 'Ooh, he is brilliant.' He offered me a contract on the spot. It was a very easy decision. I had stopped studying and I was desperate for the break to see if I could become a professional footballer. I was still dogged by the question – could I do it? Being ditched from Nice didn't dampen the challenge which still burned inside me. Having the chance to sign for Toulon within days of leaving Nice was unbelievable, incredible. One moment I thought it was finished for me, yet two years later I made my debut in the first team. I was 18.

CHAPTER THREE

Le Débutant
Debutant

Rien ne réussit comme le succès
'Nothing succeeds like success'

Alexandre Dumas

Gaby Robert was the main man at the beginning of my career. I had instant respect for him. He was the man who thought I was good enough to sign apprenticeship forms. He was the man who gave me the foundations in terms of football and mentality when I was a youngster at Toulon. He was the man who told the manager of the first team, Christian Dalger, I was good enough for the top division. He pushed for me. I won't forget that.

The club had more of a family atmosphere than Nice. It was a much more spirited and friendly environment – a good ambience for me. There was an emphasis on encouragement, and from day one everyone believed in me. I was given a lot of chances, all the time. That was a refreshing change after the negative vibes in Nice. Gaby cut a frightening figure for the youngsters at Toulon. He wasn't

25

the type to shout and rant, but he had a certain coolness and wisdom that inspired respect. The kid he taught hasn't forgotten his lessons.

I lived in an apartment near the sea and I took the bus every morning to go to training because I was too young to have a driving licence. Every day I would go home for lunch with my friends. It was a different life and I was more than contented. But I never forgot that my first objective was to become a football player. Sometimes young lads, with an apartment, a girlfriend and a healthy dose of freedom, get carried away and forget what they are actually trying to achieve because they are too young to focus on one special thing. I had all the bonuses – apartment, girlfriend, independence – and I lived it up, but I never ignored the fact that my first challenge in life was to sign as a professional player. The dream came true after two years. When the chairman said those all-important words, 'David, I want you to sign a professional contract,' I was ecstatic.

Dalger was a big influence because he gave me my break; he had enough faith to put me in the team for my first professional game. At that stage I was playing for Toulon's second team, who were in the French Third Division. Dalger needed a midfield player because some-one was injured. He went to see Gaby Robert and asked if he had anyone suitable in his team. The reply was, 'If you need someone, take David. He is brilliant now. You have to put him in the team.'

I remember Gaby came to see me, saying, 'Your time has come, David. Maybe tomorrow you will train with the first team.'

'What?' I was taken aback and looked at him in utter disbelief. He reiterated the news I had been working towards hearing for two years: 'Tomorrow you will train with the first team because you are playing next weekend.'

Wow! It was an important turning point. I phoned my parents to tell them the news. It was a very special moment, the culmination of all our hopes.

I was a substitute against Metz, my first taste of the First Division coming shortly before the end of a 2–0 victory to Toulon. But I prefer to date the kick-start of my career from my first appearance in the starting XI – it was a much more prestigious game, so do you blame me? We played Bordeaux, who were unquestionably the best team in France at the time, boasting the talents of international stars Alain Giresse, Jean Tigana and Thierry Tusseau. I was 18 years old, standing in the tunnel, facing a 10-second walk from the dressing room to the pitch which seemed like a hike to me. I could hear the noise of the crowd reverberating. Bloody hell! I was trembling with excitement. We lost 3–0, but the experience of being out there was fantastic. I played on the right side of midfield. Dalger told me to concentrate and keep an eye on Tusseau. Afterwards all the journalists were interested in my performance. All the talk was of the debutant, a young, skilful Toulon player. From then on, I was in the first team for ever.

Two years after Nice had released me, I played against them as a professional for Toulon. I was very proud. I hadn't played too many times in Nice's Stade du Ray, and I stuck my chest out as I walked onto the pitch in another team's colours. It was a thrilling moment. I was stronger, more macho. I scored a goal and then made an assist for the decisive goal in a 2–1 win. It was phenomenal. Nobody recognised me at first. After the game the chairman came up to me and said, quizzically, 'David?' There was a very famous Yugoslav player, Nenad Bjekovic, who was the manager of Nice at that time, and after the game, he held a big meeting with everybody in the club and ranted: 'It's incredible! It's unbelievable to develop someone for four years, turn him away, he goes to another club and he is making the sun shine for them. It's unbelievable! To spend all that money, let him go and two years later he's beating us . . .' It was a huge victory for me against the people who didn't believe in me. What a great sensation: David 1 Doubters 0!

I was called up to play for the France Under-21 team. In a beautiful twist of fate, I was reunited with the man who bought me my first pair of boots. The coach was Marc Bourrier who, when he was the manager of Association Sportive Maximoise years before, obtained a tiny pair of football boots for René Ginola's little boy. I still have those boots, they are as long as my fingers, with miniscule studs. We keep them at home along with my wife's first pair of ballet shoes. Marc was a very good friend of my father and I was mates with his son, Jean-Marc. We used to play together at three years old when we were finding our footballing feet and our fathers were playing for real. So I had that extra motive to play well when I was given my international break for the Under-21s. It was a happy moment for both families.

I pulled on the famous blue shirt of France for the first time in the annual international festival of Toulon, a tournament for Under-21s. For two years running I repre- sented my country in that competition, and both years we won. The first time we beat Bulgaria in the final, and I was voted the best player of the tournament. (More of Bulgaria later, they would return to haunt me with a vengeance.) The second time we played against England in the final. Their stars were Paul Gascoigne, David Rocastle and Michael Thomas. We won 4–3. The organis- ers wanted to choose me again as player of the tourna- ment, but they gave the award to Michael Thomas instead because they didn't want to honour me in two consecutive tournaments. I played very well but they gave me another trophy, so I bear no grudge to Michael Thomas!

I remember David Rocastle kicked me in the head when the referee turned his back, because whenever I received the ball I played with some skills on the pitch which England couldn't cope with. The following year the French national team played a friendly against Arsenal and Rocastle was interviewed on French TV. He said: 'I want to say hello to my friend David Ginola, and I don't understand why he doesn't play in this team because he is the best player in France. I really want to play against him because he is brilliant.' I didn't see it but my father called me and said, 'David Rocastle spoke about you on the TV.' That made me smile.

Toulon was an ideal stepping stone for me. It was a gentle introduction into the world of professional football. We were a mediocre team, never challenging but never struggling either. I was able to play in the First Division without feeling too much pressure, and with the added advantage of having the anonymity to be a bit wild off the field. I lived my life like a kid, always having a good time. In the summer when we began to train for the new season, it was 35 degrees. We had a session in the morning, went to hang out on the beach at lunchtime, and when we returned to the training camp in the afternoon we had sand in our feet from the beach. In the evening there was always a party by the sea. It wasn't really the beginning of my professional life. It was almost amateur. Toulon was a little team and I was too young to understand the life. It was only when I went to Paris that I realised what the life of a professional was really like.

In my second season Toulon played against Matra Racing in Paris. They were managed by Artur Jorge, who was the Swiss coach in Euro 96. It was a big club with a host of great players. Matra was the chic club in France at the time. Artur Jorge had told his chairman when I was

20 that he wanted to sign me. He called the club, and as Toulon are always struggling financially, transfers were essential to their survival, so they agreed to sell me. I signed for Matra Racing and it was a huge step in my life. I went from Toulon, with the sea and the beach, to the capital of France, the big city. A very different life. Welcome to the big time, David.

While I was in Toulon I was making a name for myself, but I always had new challenges on the horizon. My first challenge was to sign a professional contract, second to sign a contract with a big team, third to play for the national team, fourth to win the championship and the cup. Now I have gone to play in another country. I have done everything. It's why I often think I am a lucky man. But I worked hard for it and I always set higher and higher goals.

CHAPTER FOUR

La Réalité Mord
Reality Bites

How many roads must a boy walk down
Before you can call him a man?

Bob Dylan, 'Blowin' in the Wind'

Initially, I was extremely sad to leave Toulon — who wouldn't be after such an enjoyable environment? — but I was also very excited to play in a superior team with much better players. It was a combination of exhilaration and apprehension. I knew it was going to be very difficult, aged 20, to impose myself in such an accomplished team. I was young and Matra had many experienced players at the club, one of whom was Luis Fernandez, the France midfielder, who would later be my coach at PSG. I needed some maturity. It was hard, but I had nurtured enough confidence to hold a place as a first team regular from the beginning. I was in the team for the opening match of the 1987-88 season and I played 34 games that year out of 38, while some of the older players were left on the bench. I proved that you

31

can be young and be better than more experienced players.

During my first season with Matra I did military service. In France it is compulsory, you simply have to serve your country, and everyone views it as important to do so. If you refuse, people look down on you. They think you don't like your country, that you aren't very patriotic. It's a 12–month stint, but I was in a very special battalion for professional sportsmen. We were at army base from Monday 4pm until Thursday 4pm, and then we had the whole weekend off to play our sports. It was quite flexible, so if we had a game in midweek, we were allowed to stay at the club and didn't have to go back to the army. But, like everyone else, I had three weeks in the forest with a backpack and a gun. I enjoyed it. We spent 15 days in India, 12 days in Zaire, 10 days in Morocco, which was brilliant. I had good friends there, all professional players who played together for the military team but for different club sides. Every weekend we played against each other, but in the week we were very close. I had to have short hair in those days and I laugh when I look back at pictures of me in uniform.

When I was in the army I didn't think it was particularly positive. I am not turned on by holding a gun and I get no joy from war games or the shine-your-shoes mentality. But now, when I realise what I did, I can see how much I benefited. If you haven't grown up before, you grow up in the army. It hardened me up a little bit more.

Matra was testing at first. Not only did I have to adjust to a big club with great players, I also had to find my way around the city. Paris made bustling little Nice look like it was a city on valium. For a Southerner to move to the capital is something else. When I signed for Matra it was like changing country. Moving to Paris for the first time, I felt like some peasant going to the big city. I imagine it is

the same for Geordies going to London for the first time.
You are surprised by the life – the rush, the traffic, the
crowds of faceless people, the sheer size, and, of course,
the culture, the bright lights and the unique flavour of a
24-hour city. I wasn't really prepared for my new life. In
football you have no time to adapt. People want results
yesterday. One thing Luis Fernandez said to me really
opened my naive Southern eyes. I had only just arrived at
the club. I was in the car park and he had a Porsche. I
watched him as he drove into the car park. He asked me:
'Do you like my car?' Of course I did.

'When you have this sort of car, then you are a success
in your life,' remarked Fernandez.

He looked down on me. I was taken aback by his riposte.
He had asked me a question. Did I like his car? Yes, sure I
did. His answer was so poor. It was an example of a way
you shouldn't behave in your life. What an appalling
attitude for an experienced pro to show an aspiring youngster. Totally unnecessary. What was he trying to prove?
Maybe he felt threatened by the precocious young whipper-
snapper who had arrived from lowly Toulon. In the pre-
season training sessions, Artur Jorge made two teams for
training: the players who would start the championship
took on the reserves. Fernandez was a reserve and I was
in the team with the people who were going to play.

A few years later, in my final season at Paris Saint-
Germain when Luis Fernandez was my coach, I bought
my Porsche. I arrived at the training ground and said, 'I
have success in life now.' It wasn't a big deal. I was just
trying to say you're not such a good guy, Luis. He was
always trying to shoot people down. I think it's better to
encourage young people. You can't say something like that
to someone younger than you. It's a terrible example.

The difference between Toulon and Matra was the difference between a club trying to survive and a club trying

to win things, like comparing Bolton with Manchester United. Professionally, I was much more focused. I had to concentrate more, all day. I woke up and my mind was immediately centred on the training ahead. There was more pressure and I had to be more aware of my responsibility. I had to give my best all the time, whereas if I didn't give my best all the time in Toulon, it wasn't so important.

The normal day at Matra was a long one. What I had been used to in Toulon didn't prepare me for it. My old routine – I took my swimming trunks to training and was free to go to the beach, hang out with my girlfriend, just have fun afterwards – was a total contrast to the Paris philosophy, which could be summarised in two words: work hard. But I had no qualms about it because I had a more serious objective. I had to prove to Artur Jorge that I could play in this team. I wasn't guaranteed a place. I knew I would be in the squad, the reserves, maybe a sub but I had to prove I was worth a place in the first XI. I did, but I hadn't had to think about this problem in Toulon.

We had a bad time at Matra. The first season was difficult – there wasn't a very good atmosphere in the team, which was something I wasn't used to and I didn't much care for. Artur Jorge left the club in heart-rending circumstances, as his wife was very ill. The reins were taken by his assistants, but they didn't have the experience and managerial flair that Artur exuded. Things went from bad to worse. The chairman of Matra Racing decided to pull out his finances. Matra is a huge electronics company in France, and the chairman didn't have the patience to wait for his team to be successful.

In my second season there, the 'Matra' was dropped from the team name and we played as Racing Paris. By now we were all young lads, after an exodus of the big stars following the withdrawal of sponsorship. There was one highlight; we played in the final of the French Cup in 1990, having beaten the mighty Marseille 3–2 in the semi-final, in the Velodrome. They were playing in the European Cup and we were such underdogs that mongrels would have been rated with more of a chance! It was a result which confounded the experts. We had a big party afterwards. The odds against us winning must have been 100-1 and I don't think anyone put their money on us! Quite brilliant. In the final we played against Montpellier, who had Cantona in their team. We lost. In the end it turned out to be a very poor season. Although we had a good run in the Cup, the biggest disappointment wasn't the fact we lost in the final but that we were relegated.

I didn't want to play in the Second Division and the club had money problems and had to sell several players. It was time for David Ginola and Racing Paris to part company, for our mutual benefit. I was sold to Brest. A new adventure, a new area, a new life. Brest is in Brittany, in the North of France. When I began to play football I planned to draw a geographical line at Paris, I had no intentions of going any further north. And here I was in Brest, the same weather as Newcastle! But in footballing terms I had no complaints. The first season was brilliant. We played really well, we were top of the league for four months, and we finished sixth. We were a very young team, the France goalkeeper Bernard Lama and midfielder Correntin Martins were thriving in the promising side we had. I have happy memories. I had a good time with my wife. It was very different to Paris. The life in Brest was incredible. The people were very passionate, very warm.

To be honest, when I signed I didn't expect I would be so happy there, so it came as a pleasant surprise. It wasn't a town I was looking forward to living in and I arrived to find something great. Having got used to the excitement of living in Paris, with the full range of activities and amusements which is the heart and soul of the capital city – restaurants, theatre, concerts, museums – I led a very simple existence in Brest, but I was far from bored. It's a poor town and there are precious few diversions, in fact it's famous for its potato fields! Because of this environment the players developed a very close bond and rewarding friendships flourished. There was nowhere chic to go out and nothing captivating to do (once you've seen one potato field you've seen them all) so we revelled in fine parties at someone's house all the time. It was in Brest that I first struck a connection with Bernard Lama, still a great friend to this day. We were room-mates. I have fond memories of the hours we spent staying at the team's training camp before games. We sat outside on the balcony, watching the sea and chewing the fat with the sound of Bernard's reggae music setting a perfect backdrop.

I was selected to play for the French national team for the first time when I was at Brest, for a European Championship qualifying match against Albania in Tirana in 1990. It was the first time that any Brest player had been selected for the national team. Brest was a small club, like Wimbledon. I never dared to dream I might be called up. A player from Brest never gets selected for the French squad. Never! I remember the scene very clearly. When the call came I was at a training camp in this little place in the middle of nowhere, we were all sitting round the table having dinner. The phone rang and the trainer Slavo Muslin went off to answer it, had a little chat and then came back to the table and announced, 'Right boys, I've got some good news . . .' I was just sitting there eating, we all were. 'David has been selected for the French national squad.' I practically choked on my soup. I looked up and asked, 'Come on, are you joking or what?'

'Absolutely not,' was the reply. 'That was Michel Platini

on the phone. He has just told me he has selected you.' My heart just went boooom. All the players gave me a standing ovation. It was brilliant. Platini was my idol. He was probably the best player to have ever come out of France, the only French footballer who is known throughout the world. He was a player unlike any other. There's only a few in that class – Maradona, Pelé, Cruyff, Beckenbauer and Platini. They are the exceptional players, each with unique gifts. As football players, we are not really in the same league as those guys. They are the peak you can be in our profession.

I arrived at the national team headquarters, the wide-eyed new recruit. There I was among all the stars. I felt like a child who had discovered the world. I stayed quietly in the corner, the youngest member of the team. Michel Platini told me to think like a man. He told me to be confident, to cover plenty of ground on the pitch, and to play my normal game. After all, you are only picked for the national side on the strength of how you perform for your club.

At Brest I got into peak physical shape. *Petit* David, who Nice were convinced was too small to be a professional footballer, metamorphosed into a finely tuned athlete. There is something about the air up there, a point not lost on our coach, Muslin. He was a fitness fanatic, always urging more effort. The huge rocks in the Asterix books, similar to those at Stonehenge, are unique to the region and are shaped by the biting wind. They say the Brittany air makes you strong. It didn't do much harm for Asterix's enormous friend Obelix . . . and I suppose it didn't hinder me either.

Although Brest finished sixth in the league, we were relegated because of financial irregularities. The French Football Federation fined us and ordered that we should be demoted. Throughout the season there was a good atmosphere and we had good players but nobody had any idea about the money situation. It was all swept under the carpet. I wanted to leave. Being relegated after we had worked so hard to finish sixth – a wonderful achievement for a club of Brest's status – left a bitter taste in the mouth. I wouldn't have minded so much had we gone down on merit, or lack of it, but this was something beyond the realms of what the players do on the pitch.

Behind the scenes the club was run like a madhouse. The chairman was François Yvinec, a huge character. He gave everything he had to his club and even when it was inevitable Brest would go bust, he refused to let go. He wouldn't sell the club, and he was reluctant to sell the players. One day a delegation from Marseille came armed with a contract to buy me. Yvinec hid when they arrived and as the men from Marseille came through the front door he made his escape through the back. He wouldn't let me go. I was very frustrated. In what was to be the club's last chance of survival, Yvinec invited some friends of his into the Brest fold to help the club: Charly Chaker, a renowned wheeler dealer; Ibrahim Souss, a militant who represented the PLO in France; and Phillipe Legorju, from the French special police force the GIGN, the equivalent of the SAS. What a way to run a football club! To put it into perspective, Chaker and Souss are in jail now.

Legorju had a strange way of motivating the team. He took us on army courses, to show us how he trained his troops. We had to endure the full commando course and we all had to fire a .357 Magnum gun. I am not sure how he thought this would benefit professional footballers, but I can say you have to be rigidly strong and extremely focused to resist the recoil of the deadly weapon. He demonstrated by shooting at one of his colleagues who wore a bullet-proof vest. Watching this spectacle sent shivers through me. It was a bizarre way of preparing for the Championship.

The club was dying a prolonged, painful financial death. The only assets the club had were us, the players, but the board had no interest whatsoever in selling us. Brest needed someone to come in and invest in the club, to make it into something stable and something great. Instead, a couple of dodgy 'entrepreneurs' tried to buy the club for one measly franc. They didn't have any money, and their ploy was to get control of the club, debts and all, then wait until the end of the season and sell all the players to make a quick killing. Of course they would have murdered the club in the process. The players were really worried. As it was, we hadn't been paid for three months, and we didn't fancy our chances of collecting any wages if this devious duo took charge. The situation was so bad, we decided we had to do something about it. We appeared in front of a court tribunal to press our case. We won, the club was liquidated, and all the players were free to go. It was a few years before the Bosman ruling had allowed players to move for nothing, but we were all available on a free transfer. I had offers from every big club in France.

Poor Brest. The club was stripped of its professional status after a tragic farce.

CHAPTER FIVE

La Passion
Passion

The French will only be united under the threat of danger. Nobody can simply bring together a country that has 265 kinds of cheese.

Charles de Gaulle

I was a free agent, and I was spoilt for choice. Imagine if you had the keys to a Porsche and a Bugatti. Which do you choose to drive? I had the two biggest clubs in France hot on my trail. Half of me was enticed by Paris Saint-Germain and the other half attracted to Marseille. They both have totally different characters but they are both phenomenal football clubs. All I knew for certain was that I wanted to get back to the top level as quickly as possible. It was crucial for me to get back into the big time – to prove that I could perform on the highest stage.

It was an almost impossible choice between Paris and Marseille, but in the end I plumped for Paris because I thought I would have fewer distractions. At Marseille, with all my friends and family, the sea and my home nearby, I couldn't have worked properly. I needed to be in a place where I wasn't stretched all the time by my folks. I knew all too well that it would be easy to shun my work and chill out by the swimming pool or the beach. Hey, why not? When the sun shines and the people smile, temptation burns. I was very close to joining Marseille, my wife Coraline even went to view a house there for us.

I joined the team that everyone was talking about. PSG were the leading force in French football at that time. I left a club that had died for one that was a symbol of growth. PSG is a club with a sensational success story. It's a very young club, formed as recently as 1970. For the first decade it was largely anonymous. The club has no past, no tradition, no history. That is being written now. Paris won the League and the Cup in the early 1980s but faded from prominence as quickly as it had achieved it and it wasn't enough to establish the club on the world stage. In 1991, the TV station Canal + bought PSG and started to build a firm structure from which the club could become a powerful force. Now, it's a sporting institution, hosting rugby, basketball, boxing and volleyball teams as well as football. It's a similar situation to Newcastle assimilating the ice hockey and rugby teams into the club.

After the qualms of moving to Paris for the first time when I joined Matra, paradoxically, when I joined PSG, I was really looking forward to capital life. I had friends and favourite haunts and I knew my way around. It was great to go back there and I think I felt a bigger buzz about it than I would have done if I had gone back to the South, to Olympique Marseille. I was able to assert myself quickly.

Everybody from the South wanted me to go to Marseille, and because I turned them down I had to accept the fact that some people called me a traitor. 'You're from the South – how could you prefer to go to Paris?!' they exclaimed.

A traitor? Well I suppose my father always supported Marseille, but he didn't seem to mind, and my wife Coraline lived opposite their stadium for years. Between PSG and Marseille there is an eternal war: OM v PSG. No other clash in French football provokes so much tension. I played in a match during 1993 and there was a fight on the pitch. I would be lying if I said that was a one-off occasion. There's a striking contrast in mentality between people in the South and Parisians, and all those differences mean the contest frequently boils over. The fans make it into some kind of civil war.

Football is often compared with war. People talk about PSG v OM as *la guerre*. The battleground provides a forceful metaphor for the game: midfield generals, last lines of defence, shots raining in on target . . . But there is too much irrational hatred in football. It shouldn't be an easy excuse for violence. Soon after I joined Paris, we had a game in Martigues, which is very close to Marseille. A lot of OM supporters took the opportunity to go to the match so they could express their feelings to me. When I was on the pitch, someone threw a corkscrew at me from the crowd. It was terrible. A couple of years later, the manager decided not to take me to the game in Martigues, a club whose fans are the most violent in the South. He said it was for my own good, that he wanted to spare me the hate and the heat that envelops their little ground. That made me maudlin. When I was a kid, my father took me to the football stadium because it was something fun and happy. Now, the thought of a day out at football stadia fills some people with fear. Not only that, I was prevented from doing my job because of the mindless hatred of people who don't know me.

I may have been dubbed a Judas, but according to the fans, the real enemy of Marseille is Eric Cantona, who once threw his white shirt to the ground and trampled over it when he was substituted, which was seen as being utterly sacrilegious and unforgivable. The fans worship that shirt. You can kiss the shirt, you can clasp it like a flag or a trophy, but you can't do something like that with the shirt of Marseille; it was a very grave mistake. Anyone who did the same with the shirt of Newcastle would be construed as the ultimate traitor (or a Sunderland supporter). What made it worse was that Cantona comes from Marseille. Imagine what the Geordies would think if Lee Clark or Steve Watson ripped the black and white shirt from their back, threw it to the ground and marched over it.

In Paris they don't have the same affection for the shirt which is symptomatic of the clash of culture. In St Maxime, although it isn't the number one fashion symbol, you could walk around wearing a Marseille shirt and no one would call you an idiot, but in Paris it's absolutely unthinkable and everyone would regard you as a peasant.

Ultimately, I was fortunate to have chosen PSG, because otherwise I might have been caught up in the Marseille bribery scandal. They were found guilty of trying to rig a match against Valenciennes by bribing three opposition players, so they would take it easy in the league match which took place a week before the European Cup final. They were severely punished by the football authorities when it later came to light. UEFA banned them from European competition and the French Football Federation demoted them from the First Division, banned the president Bernard Tapie and his assistant Jean-Pierre Bernès, and stripped them of their League title. The records show no winner of the 1992-93 championship. To make matters worse, Marseille won the Second Division in their first year of exile, but the authorities wouldn't allow them back into the First Division. There is a commission in France who have the power to relegate a club or deny them promotion if the club is in a poor financial state. In France there has been a lot of running off the rails in accounting of football clubs and Marseille was the worst case. The bigger the club, the closer they are scrutinised, especially from a financial point of view. Maybe Marseille could have covered it up for a year or two, but in the end they were always going to get their come-uppance.

It does French football a lot of harm when its best club goes down. Everything is optimistic for five years, then it takes a dive, then it comes back up and then takes a dive again. What the French game needs is a bit more consistency and stability and not this ridiculous rollercoaster ride.

Personally, when it all broke I wasn't that surprised. But it still hurt because, if you are from the South, you're in love with Marseille . . . Olympique Marseille, OM, is the dream of the South. It's all you hear, all you see, all you read – OM, OM all the time. The club is a legend, an institution. There is immense passion. Their fans are the most rousing in France when they mass into their home, their fiery theatre, the Stade Velodrome. 'I am proud to be Marseillais' is the slogan of the fans. Every kid from the South supports them because they are the biggest club in the region and they have a tremendous following. There is always a buzz around the club.

Had I gone to Marseille, I am certain I would have felt the same disillusionment as all the other players. It was a travesty for the team, because on the pitch Marseille were the pinnacle of French football. They won the French championship, the French Cup, and the prize that glittered brightest of all (and was therefore tarnished the most), the European Cup. The scandal damaged the players, the supporters and the whole region. Such a sordid affair wounded everyone very much. It was a kind of disaster. I remember, in this part of France, people would get up and follow Marseille, physically as well as spiritually, all over the world – Munich, Moscow, Milan . . . It was the centre of the earth for the fans and it was incomparably shamed.

When I joined PSG, I was reunited with Artur Jorge. He recommended my name to the chairman of PSG, saying he didn't believe there were any players like David Ginola in the squad at Paris. Jorge had been my coach at Matra for one season while I was there, but he lost his wife and left to try to cope with his personal tragedy. Time went by and he had to get on with his life, so he went to PSG, and he came for me as soon as he could. He told me he had watched my progress from afar. His call was irresistible. What most delighted me was that he noticed the change in me, after two years of development. When I arrived at PSG he remarked, 'You are a grown man now, eh?'

He wasn't somebody who spoke often, but he had a very eloquent manner. When he looked at you it said more than words. He is quite introverted and every time I did something which impressed him he would simply look to his assistant and puff his cheeks out in acknowledgement. That was enough. Sometimes a little pat on the back is more effective than a thousand words. Sometimes you don't need more than a ruffle of the hair.

I learned a lot from PSG, more in terms of mentality than football. I acquired a lot of experience on the pitch because we played many great teams, but the deeper benefit was maturity. Best of all, I managed to achieve tangible success. After so many years of yearning to win something, holding a trophy for the first time was a real high. My first touch of silverware came courtesy of the French Cup in 1993. I felt vindicated; finally, I had done it. I can't say every day has been a piece of cake, but for all the crumbs along the way, this symbolised that it was all worth it. It just shows, if you really want something in life you can get it. Believe in yourself.

I definitely lived my best footballing years at PSG. The proof is in all the medals we won. Everything that I had ever hoped for was realised at PSG. All the things I dreamed of achieving when I was a small boy. When you start a job, and little by little you make progress and develop, that is what happened to me at PSG. With each year, things got better and better, new experiences, new goals and new achievements. When you're a footballer you dream of winning all these things and when it suddenly started happening, one after the other, boom, boom, boom, you say to yourself: 'Well, I really chose the right career. This was no mistake.' I'd waited for ages for the bus and then three arrived at once. We had such a great team spirit. To create a really good team, the players have to be mentally in tune with one another. For three and a half years we lived some incredible times, and even for some of the players who didn't particularly have much in common, with all the victories and momentous occasions we had, they forgot any animosity and found a common bond.

There was never a dull moment. My years at PSG were full of memorable events. When we won the championship for the first time in the season 1993-94, after the euphoria of the last game we all headed for the Champs Elysées. The police blocked the street off especially for us and it was jammed with our supporters celebrating. It would cause the same mayhem if Piccadilly Circus in London was closed. We had a big party in a famous restaurant called Fouquet's. We stood looking out of the first floor windows, virtually hanging out, and there were thousands of fans outside on the Champs Elysées. It was a visual feast; the road was one huge mass of rejoicing people and the blue and red of PSG. What a dream! I remember one of the young players, Francis Laccer, hoisted me onto his shoulders. He was impressionable and he looked up to me. He beamed and shouted, 'You are the star. It's your title.' We cheered and sang with the fans. I have a warm glow inside when I think about it now. It was a breathtaking scene. Incredible!

Our performances in Europe were remarkable. We were semi-final losers three years running, losing out to Juventus, Arsenal and AC Milan respectively, who all went on to win in the final. But our European adventures proved to be exhilarating experiences, with quarter-final victories against Real Madrid and Barcelona being particularly dizzy highlights. Little compares with crucial games on a magnificent stage, with mounting suspense and adrenaline-filled atmospheres . . .

To play majestic football and score a glorious goal is quite a moment in that situation. I will never forget our UEFA Cup encounter with Real in 1993. It provided the game when PSG established themselves on the European stage. We were a young club, and we proved to the world we were a force to be reckoned with. The tie proved to be momentous for me too. We lost the first match in Spain 3–1, but I scored the goal which gave us a lifeline, a strike which caused shockwaves. I was christened 'El Magnifico' by the Spanish newspapers. Nobody gave us a chance to make up the deficit in the second leg – we were lost causes. At the return in the Parc des Princes, everything clicked and we ran out 4–1 victors, with goals from George Weah, the Brazilian Valdo, my friend Kombouaré, and one from me. We went berserk. What made it so sensational was catching up from a seemingly impossible position. What we achieved felt amazing. A comeback like that was almost unimaginable, but we did it. Madrid was one of the most incredible matches I have ever played in.

Two years later, we faced the mighty Barcelona in the European Cup quarter-finals. They were managed by one of the players I admired since childhood, Johan Cruyff. I watched him, the maestro of Ajax and Holland, the artist of football, on television with my father. Oh, to see such a genius on the field. He taught me from afar that football is poetry in motion. I remember when Holland lost the World Cup final to Germany in 1974, I was sad in my little corner of France. It was a special moment for me to play in front of Cruyff. Performing against his team 20 years later, I wanted him to admire me in return.

They were an impressive side – including Hagi, Koeman, Sergi and Stoichkov – but we weren't intimidated. After all, why should we have been frightened? We had won every game in our Champions League group, consisting of Bayern Munich, Spartak Moscow and Dinamo Kiev. We arrived at the Nou Camp brimming with confidence and drew 1–1, thanks to a brilliant goal from George Weah. The match was played at feverish pace with skill to match, and we carried on where we left off back in Paris. I thoroughly enjoyed the game and did my best to terrorise the Spaniards' defence. Barcelona scored a goal on the break, but we deservedly equalised through Rai and clinched the game with a late winner, a piledriver from Vincent Guerin.

You can't always celebrate these things to the level they deserve. No soirees in Fouquet's, I'm afraid. When you have a vibrant victory in Europe there is always a league game coming up a few days later. You can't afford to let yourself go completely. There is always the feeling that the players are holding themselves back, for we know we must stay relatively sane as there is an important match on the horizon.

I hope I can attain the same achievements again. The more you win doesn't necessarily mean the less you feel, and you always search for this sort of emotion again. Some people say success breeds nonchalance. But every

victory is set against a diverse backdrop; different circumstances, stadia, scorelines, suspense . . . Nothing is just a
repetition, so it's always possible to feel the same emotional impact again, as if for the first time. I want those
feelings again.

CHAPTER SIX

Les Vedettes
Stars

Moi aussi, j'ai mon image. Crois-tu qu'elle ne me donne pas le vertige?
'I also have my image. Don't you think it makes me dizzy?'

Jean-Paul Sartre

Joining the major club in the capital was a catalytic moment for me off the field. My career sped off at a tangent, away from being pure football and into another dimension. A year into my spell with PSG, I noticed the change in the way people looked at me in the street. One day you are going about your business and the next people are staring at you. Then you start to receive letters and next you appear on television. It was a gradual process, not an overnight success situation. It's a funny sensation (both weird and ha ha): you aim to become something and suddenly, a year after walking down the street and nobody turning a blind eye, people chase you and try to touch you. It's a great buzz. I worked hard to achieve something and

51

the attention I received was a symbol that I had arrived.

The level of publicity I generated developed into something more intense than anything PSG had seen before. In France there are three players who get talked about incessantly, where the interest transcends events on the pitch. Jean-Pierre Papin was the first, then Eric Cantona, then me. Wherever you go in France, even the smallest most rural village, people will have heard of Papin, Ginola, Cantona. In a way, these names have been taken out of football and put onto another plane. We are not only footballers. We are a part of everyday life and every Thom, Didier and Henri has heard of our names.

Papin's was a different story to the experience Eric and I have had. Jean-Pierre has a very positive image because he played for Marseille when they were at their peak and won four consecutive championships in France. He was the focal point of that magnificent team so he is still highly respected. Papin was simply the ace in the profession. The difference for Eric and me is that we are more marketed. That change came about because image and commercial links with multi-national companies have become an inherent part of the professional sport, and that was only just beginning when Jean-Pierre was at his peak. When I first started playing, marketing wasn't such a powerful force in football. Companies didn't put their names forward for association with footballers. Advertising campaigns didn't seek the approval of a top footballer's face. It wasn't considered to be very glamorous.

Now, if you're not seen in the media, you're nothing. I know company directors who want to get on TV because they feel their profile needs it. They might earn an absolute fortune, but if they walk down the street nobody would give them a second glance. They look at us and think: 'Who is this guy, he's a footballer, and he's walking down the street and people are falling at his feet!' They crave that type of attention and will do anything to get on TV. They would like to be recognised the way we are but, ironically, we would like to walk down the street occasionally without people pawing at us and asking for autographs. Just sometimes it would be a pleasure to go shopping with our families without being recognised!

Of course, I didn't become a football star to be acknowledged in the street, but now I am one I have to accept the fact that people want to see me. It's important not to lose track of the fact it's only down to my football talent, nothing else. But once you have this popularity, it gets taken over. As soon as you start to climb the tree of publicity, you lose control over whether you are going to stay on the branch of football. That happens because of other pressures, from the media attention in particular, and it has little to do with football.

Every now and then it all becomes a little bit invasive. For example, I couldn't believe the coverage when my house in Newcastle was burgled during the close-season. It was absolutely everywhere in England: David Ginola's house was burgled! On teletext, TV, newspapers . . . I don't really think the general public needs to know that. Reporters from the English tabloids even tracked me down to my house in France when I was on my holiday. But you have to know what you want in life. If you are content to stay a small-time, regular football player, you don't have to put up with it, but if you have chosen the life of a big star, you have to take it as part of the package.

How far can you keep the private life of a star from being public property? The media love nothing more than a star who has been seen gambling or womanising or indulging in too much alcohol or drugs. You can't judge people. Everybody should be able to do what he wants as long as he respects everyone else. Somebody who is in the public eye can no longer do what he wants. The media is a powerful moral tool. I can't always go where I like, or do what I like. That's the mentality.

The star system is a volatile animal. When someone is unknown, the media don't know how they will react to interviews and a camera being pushed in their face. It is a 50/50 chance whether they will clam up or be naturally expressive. Essentially, it's a totally random business. At the same time, the media can craft an elusive quality around any individual if they want to. Stardom can be easily manufactured. It's like having a basket of eggs on the table and they pick one out, and say, 'OK, this is the one we will take to the very top.' Later, they might decide they don't want this egg any more and they drop it without any scruples, then simply return to the basket to pick up a different one. The day they don't want you, they will let you go and start with somebody else. If you are in the public eye, you can be inflated and deflated equally quickly. But it doesn't really bother me because I started off a nobody. I was nothing and I have become something, so obviously I'll try to make it last as long as possible, but if I have to go back to the land of obscurity, I won't mind. Stardom is an illusion. It can appear and vanish as quickly as a rabbit in a hat.

So why did they choose David Ginola? It's very simple. When you are in Paris, you are surrounded by the media. All the journalists, all the TV stations and radio networks are based there, and each time they need a guest or an expert for a show, you are right on the spot. I suppose the fact that I was approached a lot might have something to do with the fact that I look OK and I come across quite well on the TV.

France is lagging a bit behind England regarding commercial opportunities for footballers. Every player in France has an agent, but for the majority of players, the agent's sole purpose is to converse on their behalf with

Ginola exhausted after training. (*Action Images*)

The good, the bad and the ugly. (Left) Clinching the 1995 cup double; (above) the nightmare of France v Bulgaria, November 1993; and (below) in agony, thanks to Marseille. (*Sipa/Colorsport, Presse Sports/Action Images* and *Marc Francotte/Popperfoto*)

At leisure. (Above)
With Coraline and
Andrea, and (below)
with a pint.
(*Sipa/Colorsport* and
Temp Sport/Colorsport)

At work. (Above) In action at
St James' Park, and (below)
modelling for Cerruti. (*Ben
Radford/Allsport* and *Presse
Sports/Action Images*)

The horror unfolds – sent off against Arsenal in the fifth round of the Coca-Cola Cup on 10 January 1996. (*Action Images*)

Ginola celebrates his first goal for Newcastle, against Sheffield Wednesday on 27 January 1995. (*Action Images*)

Words of wisdom from Kevin Keegan (*Action Images*)

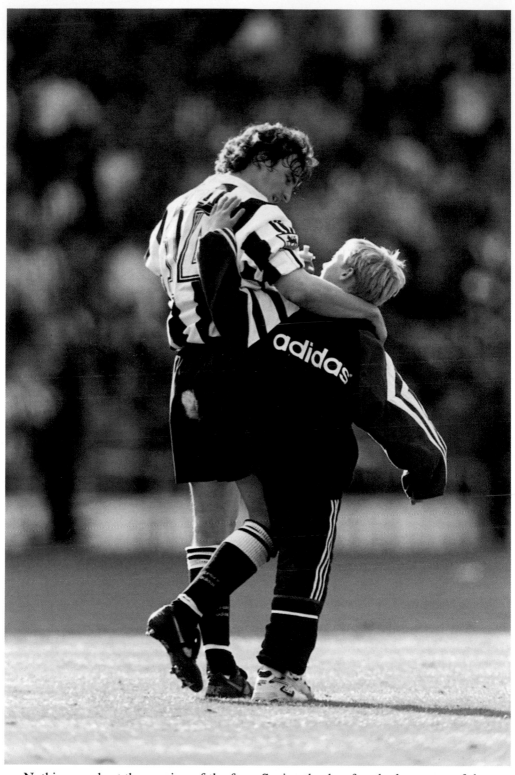

Nothing can beat the passion of the fans. Saying thanks after the last game of the 1996 season. (*Stu Forster/Allsport*)

football clubs. There is a fundamental difference between the management of an ordinary professional compared to a player who is a darling of the media. When you enter into the star system, having an agent who negotiates your contract with your club and deals with any transfers is not enough. I needed someone who could handle extra-curricular business opportunities, who had a good understanding of this booming market for footballers. Dominique Rocheteau, once known as St Etienne's Green Angel, had been looking after me. Rocheteau suggested I should meet Olivier Godallier because he felt he himself didn't have the expertise and experience in marketing (although he surely had it all when it came to football). Olivier and I hit it off straight away. He told me that there were a lot of worthwhile things I could be doing. These days having someone who can deal with sunglasses companies, clothes designers, advertising men and the media is just as important as someone to negotiate with a football club. Olivier takes a lot of the steam away from me. He knows what interests me and what doesn't and he is selective on my behalf. That's a big advantage for me. I don't want any old crappy company driving me crazy about working together, so they drive Olivier crazy instead!

Our guiding principle is that we are not going to accept anything and everything, because I have to be mindful of protecting my image, and of course I am committed to my club and it would be wrong to spend all my free time doing other work. In order to be at my best for my club, I have to rest a little when I am not training or playing. Olivier and I try to restrict it to things that are not totally inane. There are some young players who have seen myself or Eric on TV, so when they get offered some rubbish slot they accept it, just to get their face on TV because they value the exposure. But not all exposure is good exposure. The trouble is young players don't have the choice, they are afraid to turn something down. I can choose but they can't. I won't do any old thing for a royalty cheque. There are certain TV shows I wouldn't appear on. Once I was invited onto a variety show where artists take centre stage to perform. I have no place there; it's not my scene. Anyway I'm no singer. The worst thing I ever did was agree to appear on a dreadful programme hosted by an exasperating character called Christophe De Chavane. The idea is to make a fool of the guests. I just went on and basically clowned about. I had to pretend to be an aeroplane, among other things. It was just the worst. I can't say it was the most cerebral thing requested of me.

But all this peripheral activity is not only a necessary evil, it's also quite intriguing to go outside the world of football, see something else. And of course it's also a way of making money and there are perks! You get beautiful clothes given to you. That's quite a nice side to it. There are people who are jealous who might think, 'What is he doing? What kind of a way to behave is that?' But they would be the first to accept if the carrot was dangled in front of them. What's the point of saying no? If someone said to you, 'Wear these sunglasses and I'll pay you a fortune,' you'd be crazy to turn them down. I really don't see the point of saying no. Nobody's asking me to pose with toilet paper. It's not anything remotely embarrassing or difficult. All I've got to do is wear nice clothes and put a decent pair of sunglasses on my face. Big deal.

For example, I spent most of this summer doing up my new home in St Maxime. I have always rented a house there for my holidays, and this was the first time I have lived in my own house in my town. It's very exciting and it's the realisation of a dream. Over my professional career I have put aside a lot of money with this in mind. We built it from scratch and designed everything ourselves. If you look out of the window of the lounge you can see the sea, and it looks as if the swimming pool moves like a waterfall into the Mediterranean. As a footballer you live in a lot of houses, but none of them are your home. I have worked hard for it for 10 years. It's a very gratifying feeling.

Last year I bought a Porsche. When I was 18 years old I wanted to have a Porsche, but I didn't have the money. I thought, 'One day I will buy my Porsche . . .' Then, after nine years in football, I had the money so I went to the showroom and asked how much it would cost. The salesman told me, I said OK, we shook hands on it and he gave me the keys. I didn't want to get a loan and pay it off, I wanted to wait until I could actually afford it, because in my opinion, you get pleasure from something you can afford, not if you have it but you are permanently worried because you are in debt up to the neck. That takes all the pleasure away.

People can get very jealous. When I was younger, I was affected by people's comments about money or fame. It doesn't bother me now because I have my friends and I know who are the true ones, so I don't care about the rest. When people call me 'an idiot' it flies straight over my head. I've realised that people who say they hate you and they detest what you do, in fact, only hate you because they wish they were doing the same thing. In a bizarre way, sometimes your biggest detractors are somewhat perversely your greatest admirers.

I started modelling during my last season with Paris Saint-Germain. We had a meeting with the designer Nino Cerruti, and he asked me if I wanted to be a partner of the Cerruti product. We considered the pros of an alliance between Cerruti and myself and the decision to work together was an easy one. Now Nino and I are close friends. I enjoy it very much. It's a new concept in my life and it isn't too time consuming. I don't work for Cerruti every day, so it can be a refreshing change from football.

We signed the deal at exactly the same time as I signed for Newcastle. It was an exciting period in my life. I had the offer from Newcastle on the Monday, flew to Paris to do the catwalk on the Tuesday, then flew to St James' Park on the Wednesday to sign the deal. The fact I spent a few hours cruising at several thousand feet was irrelevant. I was on a high all week. I did the catwalk with two rugby players, Emile Ntamack and Laurent Cabannes, just for fun. We drank a bottle of champagne before going on because we were very nervous. Because when I go on to the catwalk, or if I play golf and have a very important putt to win the game, it's an unfamiliar sensation. I don't really want to be a model, it's not my vocation. My job is football. I know my job. I've played football professionally for a decade, so I don't get apprehensive before a game because I know what I can and can't do. I know every facet of my game. I know myself very well. It's not the same in the other things I do.

My wife has no problem with me modelling, other than the fact she would prefer not to see so many women around me! That's normal. I suppose every wife would feel the same. She's already done modelling herself when she was younger, so she knows the scene. Sometimes when she sees photos of me with supermodels like Eva Herzagova or Kate Moss, she must think . . . Well, she's got to trust me! But I know that there are a lot of women who tell her, 'I don't know how you can put up with it!'

In the public eye, I feel absolutely responsible towards young people, as they are the ones who adore and worship you unconditionally. You can't just say any old thing in front of young people who are impressionable and are going to take your opinion as gospel. I feel much more responsible towards young people because they are very naive. As that was something I suffered from myself, I am fully aware of the traps. When you know these guys idolise you, you have to be aware of the influence you have, treat it carefully, respect it. I always preach, 'When I started out as a footballer, nobody wanted me. But I kept on fighting for what I wanted and I got there.' I think that idea can be a very positive message to convey to young people. Today, life is not easy – there is a lot of unemployment, crime and poverty – and I think it's an important example to set. I didn't have an easy time either, but I managed to climb the mountain because I was determined. I didn't give up and slip to the bottom. That's a valid message for everyone, even beyond the parameters of football. I didn't cruise along a smooth road all the time or take the easy route. If someone is faced by troubles or knockbacks, and they think to themselves, 'Take David Ginola, he didn't find it that easy either and if he can do it, maybe I can do it,' that's positive.

CHAPTER SEVEN

Le Crime
Crime

Don't hate, it's too big a burden to bear.

Martin Luther King, Snr

I have one phobia in my life: sharks. I love the sea, I love dolphins but I am obsessed by sharks. I wake up sometimes in the night, sweating, after dreaming I was being eaten by a shark. My fascination for sharks was sparked by the film *Les Dents de la Mer*, 'Jaws', which I was very struck by when I went to see it. It portrays a type of death which I find totally obsessive. If I was on a boat, stranded on the open sea and you told me to swim back to shore, I would do it but I would be absolutely petrified that there was a shark behind me, out to get me. When we are on the earth, grounded, we are on our natural territory, but when we're in the water, I don't believe it is our world. To find yourself in the middle of this deep navy blue world is not for me. It's hostile.

The death I fear most is not being drowned, but being eaten by a shark. If you are eaten by a shark you die

61

before you have the chance to drown. If sharks didn't exist I would have no problem being in the sea. I love whales and dolphins and I've been diving, which opens up an incredibly beautiful world, but I can never shun this lingering fear that a shark has me in its sight. I always have this tendency, if I'm in the water, of turning round to check if there is something behind me. I saw 'Jaws' when I was quite young, having left the house without my parents' permission, and went with some friends to the cinema. I was impressionable and it got into my mind. It's a phobia I cannot shift. The only way to shirk my shark obsession would be to dive into the sea where there are millions of sharks – but I would have to be in a very safe cage!

This fascination for the sea explains why I also love the film *Le Grand Bleu*, 'The Big Blue', which is set in the depths of the sea and is based around the obsessions of a diver. I wouldn't dare to sink as deep as he does, but I find it mesmerising to watch.

In the South of France there is a waterworld park called Marineland. It's similar to Sea Life in Whitley Bay. I have no qualms when I am there because those sharks are not the same as the wild, white sharks which I fear. Man-eating sharks. In a sense they have similarities with a certain type of person who I detest, those who are out to attack, those who pounce on another human being without thinking.

November 1993. I felt like I could do no wrong. I didn't know what I had done to deserve such good fortune, but life was sweet. PSG were going from strength to strength, Coraline and I were enjoying thrilling times living in Paris, and I had forced my way into the French national squad which was as close as dammit to qualifying for the World Cup.

Everyone in France had half an eye on USA 94. With

two games to go, we held pole position in the qualifying group. All we required was a point, and we faced Israel and Bulgaria at home. As far as the public was concerned, it was a foregone conclusion that we were going to the World Cup. Against the Israelis I scored and put on my best performance in the blue shirt of France, but we surrendered the initiative and lost 3–2. The result was a shock, but at least we had another game to redress the damage.

I became involved in the intense hype which crescendoed into a frenzy during the pre-match build-up to the game against Bulgaria. There had been a lobby for my inclusion in the French team, but the manager Gérard Houllier was mindful of disturbing the attacking partnership of Jean-Pierre Papin and Eric Cantona. I made the mistake of giving an interview where I was asked if Houllier was being influenced by them. I agreed. It was what a lot of people had been saying. I stupidly believed honesty was the best policy. I learned my lesson. Fortunately, it was more of a problem in the press than it was in the team camp.

Bulgaria. The very word makes me shudder. With a minute to go we had our precious point. It was 1–1. What followed on the field was a nightmare; what followed off the field bordered on insanity. I lost possession, and seconds later Kostadinov scored with the last kick of the game and France were eliminated.

The French like to see heads roll when there is a crisis, and our failure against Bulgaria was a national crisis. They have an obsession with finding their man. As is well documented in history, we like cutting heads off in France. After all, the French invented the guillotine. A physician by the name of Joseph Guillotin invented it in 1789 and ever since then we've been chopping people's heads off. They had to find a head to roll and mine was the one they chose. Admittedly, if you try to pin the blame on the whole team it isn't as effective. You cannot make sufficient impact if you go for all 11 as the effect is diluted. You need one person to point the finger at. Once you've found your man, everyone's immediately happier. The whole situation was blown up into something that it wasn't. I think the French media were there with their airline tickets at the ready and their hotels booked, waiting to have a wonderful month in the United States. It didn't happen and somebody had to pay the price. They had to find a scapegoat. I was the net at which they shot all their frustration.

Football is a game, and we are a team of 11 players. A team. We win together and we lose together. You can make a mistake, but there are ten players on the pitch who can help you. Sitting in the dressing room after the game, I never considered what a drama I was going to wake up to the following morning. Make up your own mind. This is what happened: there was a free kick, someone passed me the ball out wide and I crossed the ball to Eric Cantona, who was unmarked in the 18-yard box. There was no one around him. There were nine players in our half. Bulgaria intercepted my cross and five passes later they had scored and France had lost the game. They said it was my fault because I crossed the ball too long for Eric.

I remember the morning after the night before, sitting at home in my lounge, upset enough anyway that we had lost and we weren't going to the World Cup. A journalist friend of mine phoned me at home and told me to switch on the television to watch what the manager Gérard Houllier was saying. I saw him claim, 'David Ginola is a criminal. I repeat, he is a criminal.' He said it twice. Make no mistake here. It's him! He wanted me ostracised. He wanted me shattered.

I overhit my pass to a team-mate. Did this warrant the

manager branding me a criminal? I am not a criminal. I have never stolen anything, I have never killed anyone, I try to be honest in my life. Everybody makes mistakes and people should be honourable enough to forgive them. Houllier's words caused national hysteria.

It was like the sky had fallen on my head. I had no idea they would accuse me. What had I done? If the media had chosen to blame me, that would have been one thing, but it's something completely different when the manager singles you out as the sole offender. I had absolutely no idea that he would say anything so vindictive. It shocked me. I always thought it was a team game. OK, it was a team problem and I was prepared to accept my part in the defeat. Afterwards the French public was divided. Fifty per cent thought it was unfair to blame me and 50 per cent agreed with the manager.

It was a bombshell, but I didn't collapse into a personal crisis – I'm a big boy and I can take care of myself. Sticks and stones can break my bones but words will never hurt me? I would be lying if I said those words caused me no pain. But what really tore me apart was seeing my immediate family – my wife, my parents, my grand-parents – hurting for me. They felt it for me. That's the hardest thing to take, to see them crying on my behalf, that's what really killed me. It's impossible to have to deal with it when the people you love phone you up and they are in tears, saying, 'What has this moron said about you?'

My next game was only four days after Bulgaria, at Toulouse. The Paris manager, Artur Jorge, asked me if I wanted to play. I had no doubts; I was playing. It's my job and I wanted to play, I owed it to my club, my team-mates, the fans and the manager. The stadium was packed and there was an electric atmosphere as the players emerged from the tunnel. Then, as I came out onto the pitch, the mood turned and everybody whistled and jeered me. I felt like the whole of town was haranguing me. It was very hard. Every time I touched the ball and tried something, they started hissing again. After five minutes, we had a corner and I scored with a header. I cried on the pitch. Not crying like a baby, but crying as a way of letting out all my frustration. We won the game.

When I scored the goal, I just felt like screaming out to the world, to let the feelings out. I had so much pent up inside me and I just wanted to let rip and scream it all away, 'Here I am! I've done it! I've scored – I can still play football!' If Houllier was there in front of me, I think I would have wanted to smash him to bits. I could have killed him from hate, not for what he did to me, but because he made the people that I love cry.

The fact that I had a stable family background helped me on the one hand, but on the other it left me unprepared for a serious knock-back. I've always been quite sensitive. I was brought up to feel respect for people. This notion of injustice and unfairness was one I didn't really come across in my childhood. I wasn't a kid from the streets; I came from a normal, happy home. If someone comes from that sort of background, and they suddenly have the kind of experience that I did, it could be a terrible shock. For a while, I had sleepless nights. But after the initial blow, I realised that any tears shed over a sporting misfortune are drops in the ocean of real affliction, like the desperation of illness or the victims of criminal abuse. There have been times when we have to grieve for football, after the tragic disasters at Heysel, Hillsborough and Bastia, where supporters died while watching the game they loved. That is worth weeping for, not an overhit cross.

My philosophy has changed. I used to say to my wife, the football comes first and then there's you! Since we got married, it's different. Now my priority is family first and football second. I've spoken to Kevin Keegan and Terry McDermott about this. They said it was exactly the same for them. When you are not married and you don't have children, football is your life. It is everything, every waking thought, every sleeping dream. But things change. I am not going to kill myself about football. When I don't play football any more, I may not earn as much money but I'll always find something else to do. And what will be left for me? I'll still have my family around me when everyone else has disappeared to find a new star to cherish. I've been playing football for ten years now and, of course, football is still my main excitement, but I know it won't be there for me forever, so my family has to take priority. Don't get the idea that I don't give a damn about my football life. I'm not putting football down. How could I? It's the beautiful game, and I get a fine living from it as well . . .

I had to find reserves of will power to stay mentally strong. It's probably because of my family that I was able to bounce back. I was fired by this need that they should think well of me. Resisting the effects of such a powerful blow was important, but not for myself. When people see me they say, 'You're OK, David. You're good looking, you've got everything.' I couldn't give a damn about that stuff. The important thing is I've got my family and when you get a bolt out of the blue like the Bulgaria situation, I was much more worried about them. I certainly didn't wallow in self pity: 'Oh poor old David, what's he going to do now after such a terrible thing happened to him.' I wanted my family to go on being able to laugh, and dream, and be proud of me. I felt that if I let it beat me, it was them I was letting down, not me.

I couldn't have dealt with people saying, 'David hasn't got any character. What can he do now? He thought he was great and he's not.' From my family's perspective, they would have thought I was a wimp! That for me was enough of a reason to pull myself together and keep fighting. It's that macho thing again. I've always had respect for the family tradition and I wanted to keep that intact. I wanted to be able to say to my parents: 'Here's the proof you brought me up in the right way. Look how I've managed to come out on top.' Imagine what it would have been like if after France v Bulgaria, people had the ammunition to goad my son: 'Your dad was a wet.' As it was, Andrea took a lot of stick which made me livid. I refused to allow anyone to photograph my son. Anything is possible with so many crazy people around, and the mood that followed Bulgaria really was insane.

I haven't seen Gérard Houllier since then. I have never spoken to him since and I never will. He quit after the Bulgaria game, to be replaced by his number two Aimé Jacquet. They are best friends. I wouldn't like to say whether that had any effect on my absence from the France squad leading up to Euro 96 and then the final selection of 22 players. Who knows? They are still very close friends and I don't know whether Houllier still considers me to be a 'criminal'.

France's next game was against Italy away, and we won 1–0, an excellent result. I provided the assist for the goal, scored by Youri Djorkaeff. It was a symbol of revenge for me. I wanted to show everybody who was against me that I still wanted to do the best I could for my country. If you are patriotic but your compatriots think you are a traitor, that is a distressing feeling, so to set up Youri's goal was my way of proving the pride I feel about representing France.

Even within the team it was 50/50, half sympathised with me and half had been indoctrinated by the outrage Houllier had invoked. It was very hard to tell who wasn't backing me. When you know people well you know they are your trusted friends, you know they are on your side. But those who are better described as acquaintances, you are never sure if they are going to smile at you to your face and put a knife in your back when you turn away.

Anyone and everyone jumped on the let's get David Ginola bandwagon. Rolland Courbis, once my manager at Toulon, gave a thoughtful tirade. As soon as I left Toulon he always referred to me as a 'woman'. Good old Rolland! He said I was a player without backbone and I didn't have a future. He said he would never again have me in his team. Since I was with PSG, the best team in France, I didn't really give a damn about that! But he taught me a thing or two about not trusting your first impressions. I met Rolland a few years later in St Tropez and I think he regrets saying that now.

After Houllier's outburst, I faced a barrage of booing and whistling on every pitch in every stadium I played at. It was like a witch-hunt. The situation reminded me of one of the lines from *L'Albatross*: 'Earth-bound, in exile, scoffed at by the crowd.' I was sick and tired of all the abuse hurled at me whenever PSG played away from home. I went to see Michel Denisot, the chairman of PSG, a couple of months after Bulgaria and said, 'I want to leave now. I can't play like this, I can't play my football in this environment.' Denisot was understanding. He sympathised, but told me to hang on in there: 'It must be very hard for you to step out onto the pitch and be subjected to booing but it will change, things will brighten up.'

It was at this time there was rumoured to be some interest in me from Arsenal, who we were due to play in the Cup-Winners' Cup semi-final. I wanted to leave PSG, but I couldn't pay all that much attention to it because I wanted to see out our progress in the championship race. A year later, their manager George Graham made another approach to try to sign me again. A lot of people were coming over and asking about me, but Denisot wouldn't sell while we were still in Europe. PSG had the semi-final against AC Milan looming. He wasn't ready to open the door to let everyone shop before he was ready. Denisot is a man with a lot of integrity. I will never forget how supportive he was after the France v Bulgaria game. He defended me and he helped me to stay strong.

As for how it feels when you come out on the pitch welcomed by a chorus of boos, well what can I say. I would rather be applauded than booed. We'd rather feel healthy than have a cold. We'd rather drive on a clear road than in the traffic. It's life and you live it. In a way, it was good for me, as it's through depressing experiences like that that you develop your character. It makes you grow. And you can appreciate good experiences all the better for the contrast. I don't take good things for granted. I know how it feels to be in the shit, so when life is sweet, I can really savour the taste.

I was defiant that I wouldn't let it beat me. I played every game from then on until the end of the championship, which PSG went on to win, the second French title in their history. After everything I had been through, I had a fantastic season in spite of it all, and the football connoisseurs held me in high esteem. I was voted Player of the Year, winning both the journalists' award and the players' award for the season 1993-94. It was an extraordinary time.

When I collected these accolades, it would have been nice for someone to come out and acknowledge it was an achievement to win in the face of such adversity. But nobody said that. Nobody. Not one of the journalists gave me any credit for surviving this dreadful and undeserved attack. Not that I wanted it for me, I had the support of my family and friends which was all I cared about, but I think it would have been a good example for people who are having a hard time. On the learning curve of life, I had virtually disappeared off the graph, but I fought my way back up.

Six months after Bulgaria, during USA 1994, the Colombian defender Andres Escobar was assassinated after scoring the own goal that ended his country's World Cup aspirations. On returning to Colombia he was gunned down. Why do people lose all rational perspective when it comes to football? I spoke to Tino Asprilla about it when he came to Newcastle. He explained there are people who say it wasn't only a question of football. The own goal was the pretext but in fact, there were rumours it was because he had stolen the wife of a guy who was influential in a Medellin Cartel. Nevertheless, Escobar's murder made me think.

CHAPTER EIGHT

Parents et Amis
Kith and Kin

When people can be so cold
They'll hurt you and desert you
They'll take your soul if you let them
But don't you let them

James Taylor, 'You've got a Friend'

Coraline is my support in the true sense of the word. She helps me to carry the weight when things get too heavy, she keeps me from falling or sinking, she gives me strength. I wouldn't have got through the Bulgaria situation, and other matches where I returned home with my heart in shreds and insults ringing in my ears, without her.

I'm an open sort of guy, I never put up a barrier. I never shut the door. It's very easy to get friendly with me, but the problem is that there are a lot of people in and out of famous circles who are very slippery. They think the fact that I'm really open with everyone is abnormal! I'm not trying to get anything out of people – I've got everything I want. There are too many people who are in the star scene for what they can get. They think the fact that I'm open is just for show. I'm pretty jovial in my outlook, but I don't think it's so clever to be distant. I don't want people to think that just because I'm a footballer I'm superior. I don't feel that way. I'm just like everyone else.

I can't stand people who twist the truth. People are always trying to put words into your mouth, read meaning into your motives for doing things. And the worst thing in life is to judge people and to read meaning into something when you don't know the person. The people who know me never try to read meaning into things I say. They say, 'David is straight down the line and he'll never stick a knife into your back.' Sometimes the people around you seem to be great guys but you never know. So it's always a bit dodgy getting involved with people these days and that bothers me. Not that someone might be two-faced, but that I am in a position where I have to be cautious.

My wife puts the brakes on for me in these situations. She warns me, 'David watch out. Maybe that's not the way you should be going. Watch who you're mixing with.' I dive right in. When it's a question of friendship I don't see the point in making it complicated and mysterious. I don't always detect when people are using me, in it for what they can get. In for what I've got, not what I am. Coraline sees this immediately.

My wife has definitely got intuition. When she sees someone coming because of what I represent, she sees it straight away. She tells me to be careful and I tell her to leave me alone! But quite often afterwards I find she was right. She says, 'I told you so, and you should listen to me. I see things from the outside. I see you and I see the people who want a piece of you. You can't see because you're in the middle of it and you've got people all around you. I live near you but not right next to you. I'm close enough to see what's going on without being involved in the circle. So I can see in people's eyes. But when you're sitting down at the table and talking to them, you have to look at everybody, yet I can see round the table and see the way they look at you. I can see whether the guy likes you for you or whether he can't look you in the face. He's only there because he likes the kudos of being at your table.'

Why don't I listen to her since she's always right? Because I don't want to fall into the opposite trap of being wary of everyone. That would be too easy. In life I always want to give everyone the benefit of the doubt. I'm not the type of person to say, just because one guy is a lowlife, everyone is a lowlife. I don't want to get into that because otherwise I'll close up and live behind a barrier. Life would probably be easier if I was a little less trusting and open, but it's not the way I am. I wouldn't be true to myself. Maybe I should try to show a little more discretion, but my openness hasn't really got me into trouble so far. Famous last words, I know.

If you really want to have problems, you have to look for them. Someone who is true to themselves has no problems. The worst thing about someone stabbing you in the back is that you misjudged them.

Compared with me, people say my wife is a closed book, a little aloof. I'm very expressive and because my wife stands back from the crowd more, people think that she is unfriendly. They don't say it to my face but I hear about it indirectly. But it's never my friends who say that. I know what she's like. If she is your friend, she is your friend for life. She's had so many bad experiences with friendship – she's been let down so many times by people who have pretended to be friendly just to get close to me – now she stands back and she's watchful. She has been deceived too many times and it's very hard indeed now to become her friend. But if you do, it's truly sincere.

Coraline and I were at primary school together in St Maxime. We weren't in the same class because I'm a year older than her. We have known each other since we were little. We sort of followed each other around without really knowing each other. When I was young I was a real boy and I wasn't at all interested in girls. I didn't even give them a second glance. For me girls were totally devoid of interest. I liked football, I played marbles, I messed around with the boys. If there was a girl who wanted to play football with us, that was all right. But if she didn't, then forget it. She may as well have not existed.

I was 19 when I met Coraline again, as an adult. I was young, playing in the reserves at Toulon. I made £150 per month – not that much to live on. So all these bitchy people who say that Coraline is only with me for my money should think again – when I first met her, I wasn't exactly earning fortunes.

She knew nothing about football. She didn't even know what it was. The only reason she was aware of it was when she went to change the channel to watch something else if her grandfather had football on TV. When I met her for the first time as an adult, naturally I asked her if she liked football. She wanted to know why I asked. I replied, 'Because that's what I want to be. At the moment I'm an apprentice.' She looked at me and said, 'What?! Quite honestly I don't see the point of these 22 idiots running around after a ball.'

I thought to myself, 'Hmmm we're getting a long way here.' But then one thing led to another. But I was quite macho about the whole thing. I made it perfectly clear to her that there was football and there was her. She could take it or leave it! We went out together for quite a long time without living together – I was in Toulon and she was in St Tropez. She came to see me at weekends.

When I went to Matra and moved to Paris we didn't see each other for a while. I came back for my grandmother's funeral a couple of months later. She knew my grandmother so, even though she didn't come to the funeral, she stayed by the car and cried when she saw it all going on. She followed me afterwards in the street and I stopped and saw her behind me, and we cried together. I said: 'Why don't you come and see me in Paris as we haven't seen each other for two months?' I met her at the airport in Paris, and a few weeks later she brought her stuff up and we started living together. We got married two years later and we've been together ever since.

I was in Disney World when my son was born. Coraline was pregnant when I signed from Brest to Paris Saint-Germain. Soon after joining, we went to Tampa Bay in America for a training trip. Coraline phoned me and told me that the baby was due on 20 January. As I was due to come back to Paris on the 18th, it seemed there would be no problem. Then the manager told us, as a treat, we were going to have a day in Disney World before we returned. I called just before we boarded the flight to Orlando and my mother-in-law said, 'David, maybe it's time now: Coraline's waters have broken. I'm going to the hospital.' But I was booked on a flight to Disney World. I was in Fantasy World in the Mexican Village, shoving as many coins as I had in a payphone to try to get some news. I had a ridiculous conversation with the operator. 'I want a number in France please. In Brest . . .' Then I screamed at my team-mates for more coins. 'Hello . . . hello. This is David Ginola, can I speak to my wife?' More coins! They said it was impossible. She was in labour.

I called back later and everything was OK. I saw my boy four days after. When I arrived at the airport in Brest, a friend of mine picked me up from the airport and took me to the hospital. He waited outside and told me to go alone, as it's a very personal moment when you see your child for the first time. I went into the lift and as it opened at the third floor, Coraline passed with the baby in her arms. I didn't want to see him for the first time in the corridor just in front of the lift, so I shouted to Coraline: 'Go into the room. I don't want to see you here!' When I arrived in the room, I finally held the baby. He was as big as my two hands. 'He's very small,' I said in amazement. 'It's normal, he's a baby,' she replied with just a hint of sarcasm. Whenever anyone asks if I was there to see the birth of my boy I can't help smiling, 'I was in Disney World.' It was a true moment of fantasy.

If Andrea is extraordinarily gifted when he gets into his teens, it would be a pity not to encourage him, but if he doesn't have exceptional qualities I would never dream of pushing him to become a footballer. I bring him up to try a bit of everything; at the moment he does golf, judo, and in fact he doesn't play much football. I'd rather it came from him.

My daughter Carla was born three years after Andrea. The thing I am most proud of is my children. You can win all the European Cups in the world but nothing is better than being a father. I always wanted to have a family. For me life is a family, like the song 'Three is a Family'. When you are married you are husband and wife, but when you have a child you are a family. My greatest fear, apart from my shark phobia, is something happening to my kids. That really scares me – it would be the most terrible thing that could afflict me.

CHAPTER NINE

La Confrontation
Confrontation

La perle est sans valueur dans sa propre coquille
'The pearl is worthless in its own oyster'

Hindu proverb

I was dealing with the aftermath of France v Bulgaria, but I wasn't the only one to suffer a character assassination during the season 1993-94. My manager Artur Jorge was another media target. They sharpened their arrows for him too. I never understood why. A strange rumour was circulating, that Paris Saint-Germain were a troubled team. We were supposedly uninspired and frustrated. What rubbish! Does this sound like the mood of a team who were accelerating towards the championship? He had built a great team at PSG, and personally, I have never been as fulfilled as I was during that season. Yet the criticism was persistent. I felt there was a consensus in the national press, intent on toppling Jorge from his perch. Why? Because he was a Portuguese who had the cheek to try to teach the French a thing or two about football. What impertinence!

Jorge was an outstanding trainer, shot down at the peak of his powers. The gun was loaded by a touch of xenophobia. The media were stupid and ungrateful. Jorge left quietly, never one willingly to create a fuss. He was above that. He left a triumphant legacy. Paris Saint-Germain were League champions. I felt great sorrow for Artur because I loved him. I missed him when he was gone and I will never forget his remarkable achievements or what he did for me.

Luis Fernandez, my former team-mate at Matra Racing, took over. The press were happier. Instead of dealing with a reserved, intellectual Portuguese they had an outspoken, dynamic, former French international. Luis had played for the national team 60 times over a period of 10 years. They thought him much more suitable for the manager of PSG. I didn't want to have any preconceived ideas about Luis based on the impressions he gave me at Matra. I simply thought: here is a new manager I am going to work with. But from day one we found it difficult to see eye to eye. It was more like eyeball to eyeball!

There was a communication problem, a personality clash. It was really hard for us to understand each other. I don't think man management was one of Luis' fortes. He had an incredible career, which gave him the self-belief to stick to his guns all the time. Luis wasn't very flexible and in his mind he is always right. After all, he always had the experience to prove it. I don't think he's a bad person, but he has very fixed views on things. He looks at things his own way. Maybe it was a 50/50 situation, perhaps both of us were in the wrong. I must confess I tend to believe I am always right too.

There was a huge contrast in attitudes: I see football as an aesthetic pleasure, as the beautiful game. Luis sees football as a conflict, as a game of guts and victories. It should have been a perfect combination – the two approaches drawn together in one side. But Luis always expected more from David; Luis was always disappointed with David; Luis never had any qualms in criticising David.

There was a lot of pressure in the camp. Negative pressure, not the constructive pressure of a team that is progressing. A level of positive stress can make you more dynamic, determined and inspired, but the PSG squad had to contend with that sticky, heavy pressure where you feel threatened rather than encouraged. There was an overriding feeling of, 'Play well or else I'll kill you!' That's quite a burden to carry onto the pitch. We had a rotten season. It was a vicious circle; we played badly and the team were fiercely criticised, we were fiercely criticised and the team played badly. And so it went on. Problems sprouted from such an unhealthy base, which had a very bad effect on the players' minds and feet. That was one of the crucial reasons for my desire to leave, because I need to have a good atmosphere among the team, a happy environment in which to play.

In the midst of all these spiteful shenanigans, the manager's biggest problem was with me. I don't really know why, but he made it clear he didn't like what I was doing with my life. Maybe it was jealousy. I remember his snobbery when I first joined Matra. He was 28, I was 20. He didn't play, I played. It wasn't easy for him to accept it. I played 34 games out of 38 that season and he played maybe four. I think I would probably accept it if I was in the same situation, but I don't know until it happens. In any case, I wouldn't take it out on the player because it is never the player's fault if the trainer decides one man is in and another out. If I had something to say on the matter I would tell the trainer. I'd try to get some sort of explanation from him. He's the decision-maker, not the young player.

Luis made it difficult for me to do some of the things I do outside of football. We had some disagreements over it. He suggested I was too involved off the field to be able to concentrate on my football. Not that it took much for him to criticise me. What a footballer does in his own time off the field is his own business. It's not that those activities are really important to me, but it is part of my life. For a manager in France it's not every day you have to deal with a player who has marketing contracts outside football. It's entirely different to the situation in England. With Kevin Keegan it's the reverse, he is happy for us if we have the opportunities. But in France there are only two players who are big business off the pitch – Eric Cantona and me. The rest just play football. That's the problem. Some people might say I spend too much time thinking about the things I do off the pitch, but that's not true. We have what we have outside football only because we play well on the pitch, and if you forget that, you lose everything.

The rift with Fernandez reached crisis point when he offered me the captaincy of PSG. The captain before me was a friend, Paul Le Guen, a man I respect a lot. When Luis decided to give me the captaincy, I felt a little awkward. I went to see Paul and explained that it wasn't my decision and that it shouldn't affect our friendship, but in a way, I would have preferred it if everything had been left the way it was – Paul as captain and myself as a player in the team. Luis said that giving me the captaincy would add an extra dimension to my game, but I don't think I am a natural leader.

Nevertheless I was captain, and, obviously, I tried to do the job as best I could. Everyone has a certain professional pride and honour when they lead the team. But no sooner than I had the armband, Luis started to play games with it. Sometimes, about three minutes before the end of a match he would substitute me. I wouldn't object normally, but a captain is the last to leave the ship and if the guy wants to change you he should pull you off 20 minutes before the end or at half-time, but three minutes before the end?

It happened once, twice, three times and I couldn't understand his motives in doing this so close to full time. Then, worst of all, during a European Cup match against Spartak Moscow, in front of 6 million TV viewers, three minutes before the end of such a prestigious match, the number 11 appeared from the touchline on the substitute's board. I couldn't comprehend what he was trying to do, and I was so frustrated I flipped. When I got to the bench I called him every imaginable name under the sun, and a few more for good measure. His response? 'OK, you go and train by yourself, and you're not playing with the team any more.'

But he couldn't easily do that to me as the fans would not understand why I was out of the side. He wasn't in a position to treat me like this. I was somebody to be reckoned with in the public eye. Deep down he knew he couldn't get on without me; I was a crucial cog in the team if it was going to function properly. He backed down and continued to pick me to play but our relationship was awful. Every day I arrived for training with a smile on my face and every day he managed to say something, or do something, to bring me down.

I wanted to leave Paris because of the bad atmosphere between me and my manager. It had been brewing over the course of the year and I decided I would have to leave at the end of the season. The time was right to move on. The feud had plummeted to such depths it wasn't possible to continue.

The problems in Paris were escalating out of hand. In

the end, it wasn't just a personal clash between Luis and me. There were other people who were secretly glad to see the problems we were having, people who would deliberately put an extra spanner in the works, not to mention hammers and screwdrivers. Certain individuals were jealous of the attention I received as a matter of course. They bitched, 'David's got everything.' Whenever I arrived at the training ground or at the stadium, there were always journalists everywhere crawling around and they wanted to talk to me. They weren't particularly bothered about the others' opinions or even, sometimes, they preferred to talk to me rather than to Fernandez. But I've always been aware not to leave others out, to act as if there was no difference, no fan favouritism. It wasn't me that put myself on a pedestal. But I could hardly tell the journalists who turned up to see me to go away. You have to respect they have a job to do as well.

It was a similar situation to the NBA, when people come to see Michael Jordan rather than any other player. There was more jealous talk than there were footballs kicked. Friends and hangers-on of other players that came to the club would sneer, 'What is this? David is the only one who matters?' The others were getting a bit pissed off. But they never said anything about it to my face, only behind my back. Nobody came straight up to me.

The atmosphere was so thick you could have cut it with cotton wool. It was reassuring to have people like Bernard Lama and Antoine Kombouaré around. They were like my soulmates and I knew they wouldn't get involved in all this bullshit. I have known Bernard a long time and we have a very special rapport. We played together at Brest, and enjoyed some merry moments there when we were room-mates. Bernard is like Bob Marley. He's very cool. I knew I could rely on Bernard. He knows my qualities, as a footballer and a man. And I know his. We had a very

normal relationship, never any problems. He loves football
and doesn't care about those other things. He knows it's
different for a goalkeeper anyway. I was close to Antoine
Kombouaré, my partner in crime. Well, my golf partner
and my companion for blues concerts. It was only the
black guys who had this really cool attitude and didn't
harp on about the fact there was yet another article about
David Ginola.

It was the black guys in the team who were behind me.
They were on my side because they liked me and they
didn't give a damn about publicity. They were only interested in the human level. I think they realised that it
wasn't that easy to be in the situation I was in. We did
have some special moments together, our friendship was
above all that media hype and petty jealousy and power
struggles. We'd go and have a drink together, only fun, no
pressure. Antoine also had problems with the manager at
PSG. He wasn't given the chances or the respect he
deserved. When I left he looked really sad. He told me
PSG wouldn't be the same without me. I missed you, too,
Antoine.

The most important lesson I have learned in my life is
humility. To be honest with yourself also means being
honest with others, to fight for what you believe in and,
above all, to remember who you are. You should never
take anything for granted, you have to realise that anything can happen, someone else's decision can change your
life. You're never in complete control, but I do believe that
you can create your own destiny. Someone who has goals
can invoke fate to help them in hours of defeat. Man uses
destiny as a sort of scapegoat to fall back on in moments of
failure. It's an easy way out. I learned this from knockbacks in general. Time teaches you this lesson. When you
are young, you make mistakes, behave like an idiot, and
when you look back you can't even believe it was you. We

mellow with age. When you're young you spend money like it's going out of fashion. Then you realise, where's all your money gone? Oh, I've spent it all just like snapping my fingers. One day I have everything, I can be rich, have women, have health; the next day, I could have nothing. I learned to stop pretending I'm someone extraordinary. I am just like everyone else. Earth calling David. Your existence shouldn't be taken for granted. It doesn't cost any more to have a simple outlook.

The last thing I would want is to look back on my time as a Paris Saint-Germain player with any bitterness. It was only in my last year at PSG that I had a problem with Luis Fernandez. My four years in Paris was the most exciting period of my life. We had great results, we played very well, there was a lot of love around me, and I became someone in my job – it was brilliant. And, in my final season, we won an unprecedented domestic Cup double.

I always had an unusual relationship with Luis Fernandez. Sometimes he even complimented me. When he was pleased with me he compared me to Garrincha, the wonderful Brazilian winger from their divine 1970 World Cup-winning team, who I used to watch on the TV. But now I laugh when I think of Luis praising me. It's not a bad compliment for Garrincha to be spoken of in the same breath as David Ginola! After we beat Barcelona to reach the European Cup semi-finals he was ecstatic and whispered into my ear that he loved me. Luis has left PSG now. I don't have any feelings about that. I don't waste my thoughts on people I don't really like. The new manager is the Brazilian Ricardo, a former PSG player and a good choice.

I knew I was going to leave France because, when you play in Paris, there is nowhere better you can go. Marseille are also a huge club, but they were still in exile in the Second Division. I had done everything I could do in

France except one thing – win a European Cup. Ironically, after three successive semi-finals, PSG won their first European trophy, the Cup-Winners' Cup, the year after my departure. I had mixed emotions. I was happy for my former team-mates and for the Paris fans, and I felt regret that I wasn't in the team to enjoy the moment, the culmination of what we had all been working towards in our European odysseys.

CHAPTER TEN

Le Pays des Geordies
Geordieland

That Europe's nothing on earth but a great big auction, that's all it is.

Tennessee Williams, *Cat on a Hot Tin Roof*

I had played my last game at the Parc des Princes in the colours of Paris Saint-Germain even though I had two years remaining on my contract. Michel Denisot, the PSG chairman, agreed to let me move. He knew I couldn't continue playing under Luis Fernandez. I have huge respect for Denisot, who is as fine a gentleman as he is a businessman. I told him I would happily stay with Paris until the end of my career, but something had to give. It was either me or Fernandez. I didn't want to put him in a position where he had to choose. He wanted me to stay, but he understood my reasons.

I spent the duration of the summer of 1995 flying around Europe to talk to a host of clubs who were interested in signing me. I spoke to a lot of clubs – Inter Milan, Real Madrid, Bayern Munich, Arsenal, Celtic – but the discussions with Barcelona were the most advanced.

I almost went to Barcelona. It took a month and a half to sort out my transfer, of which time one whole month was spent negotiating with the Catalan giants. However close I was to signing for Barcelona, I have no regrets that I did not go there then. Johan Cruyff said he really wanted me in his club. Being courted by one of the most celebrated clubs in the world, managed by one of the finest players in the history of the game is quite a humbling experience. It is a great honour for a footballer. I went for talks. They were keen for me to play there, but there was one snag: they had six foreigners on their books and in order to get me they would have to sell at least two. This was before the Bosman ruling last year changed the face of European football so there are no restrictions on foreign players.

They kept saying that I had to wait a while. I just had to hang in there until a couple of other foreigners had been offloaded. I was getting nervous waiting for them. The summer was flying by and before I knew it the season would begin and the only club I would have would be in my golf bag. To put it into perspective, the whole deal with Newcastle took three days. My agent called Barcelona and said, 'David has got an offer from Newcastle and he has to take it, because the season is approaching and he has to sort his future out.' They said, 'No, don't sign. You have to wait one more week, just one more week . . .' But we had heard that line before. It had been driving me crazy, like a scratched record for a month. We weren't prepared to wait any longer.

I almost went to Inter. However, there are so many agents and intermediaries in Italy that it became very confusing because it wasn't clear who was the right person to speak to. You have to contact one guy, and then another, and then someone else entirely before you get to the chairman. I eventually flew to Milan for a meeting with their vice-president Sandro Mazzola. I recalled with a smile how AC Milan approached my father when I was 11 years old. But for the second time in my life, I didn't quite make the move into *calcio*.

I almost went to Celtic. After initial contact at an airport in France, I went to Glasgow to see the club. I considered their offer, but my agents advised me that it might not be the best for me, because going from a club who had been playing in the European Champions League to one that was rebuilding was perhaps too much of a risk.

My priority had been to find a club which would make me happy in my football life and my private life. Of all the several clubs we had contact with in the close season, Newcastle and Keegan showed the most drive and enthusiasm. I went to Newcastle because Newcastle was the club most interested in me. You could say what brought me to St James' Park was the fact that the club wanted to have me and did everything to get me.

There had been rumours that Newcastle were keen. We had a call from a Dutch agent called Franklin Sedoc to confirm their proposal. Next stop was Amsterdam to find out more! Newcastle did everything very swiftly, a welcome contrast to all the dallying, ifs and buts that delayed all the other negotiations. Kevin Keegan was on holiday in the USA, so we spoke to assistant manager Terry McDermott and chief executive Freddie Fletcher. Their approach was almost too straightforward to be true. They made me an offer, they explained why they wanted me at the club, they told me all about Newcastle United's lofty aspirations. Simple.

I didn't know much about Newcastle. It was virgin territory for me. I knew of Kevin Keegan and Terry McDermott, famous players throughout the world. I was aware of the loyal following the club had. But I have to admit, considering Newcastle didn't have an extraordinary reputation in Europe, it was a new adventure for me.

I had been to England only twice before in my life – once when PSG played against Arsenal at Highbury in the Cup-Winners' Cup two years before, and once for a three-day shopping spree to London with my wife. I didn't know England very well, but I knew the Premiership was a good place to be. I had had some conversations with Eric Cantona during national team get-togethers. He told me a career in England is superb, the quality of the football and the clubs is brilliant, and the life outside is congenial. Of course, I knew that he was a great performer here in England. It seemed like a productive thing for a footballer to evolve in the Premiership, so even before I came here, I thought it would be a positive move for me. The English championship is part of the world's elite because there are a lot of exceptional players in very good teams and I noticed that Dennis Bergkamp and Ruud Gullit had joined the league during the summer.

Terry McDermott was very impressive in selling Newcastle United to me. He painted a purely positive picture. He told me about their meteoric rise in the last five years, that they had just bought Les Ferdinand, and they were a progressive club who should develop from a good team to a great team in the season ahead. They were expecting to book a place in European competition, and they were playing in the best possible style. He stressed that the possibilities for the club to evolve were excellent, given the amount of money the chairman, Sir John Hall, was pumping in. This would allow Newcastle to realise its potential as one of the best clubs in Europe. In any case, what won me over was the positive way everyone from Newcastle spoke to me, and their unbreakable belief that they would fulfil the club's ambitions. 'We really need you to come and play in our team, and it's a great team,' McDermott claimed. Well, every club says that! They obviously want you to think everything in the club's garden is rosy.

I chose Newcastle because I got a strong impression that everyone in the club did genuinely want me, and they gave me the guarantees I was looking for at every level: financial, professional and personal. It was all fixed very quickly and very clearly, which is the way I like things. I didn't enjoy the uncertainty about my future.

I almost went to Arsenal. It was a question of timing. Having made a verbal agreement with Newcastle, I received a telephone call from David Dein, the vice-chairman of Arsenal. He had been trying to contact me, but we kept missing each other. He finally tracked me down to our hotel in Amsterdam in the middle of the night. We spoke for an hour and a half at two o'clock in the morning, and he was very persuasive, but I had already given Newcastle my word. In the end, he regretted the fact he was too late and wished me good luck in the North East.

The next day I took a plane to Newcastle to sign a contract. We visited the club and I was delighted to see St James' Park. The proportion and condition of the stadium impressed me. Then we had an appointment to sort out the paperwork at the Gosforth Park Hotel. I met Sir John Hall, who phoned Kevin Keegan in Miami to tell him the news that I had signed. He just said to Sir John, 'It's a great deal for us.' The chairman passed me the phone so I could speak to my new manager for the first time. He said he was very pleased to have me on board and we would see each other soon for training.

I was whisked off to a press conference at St James' Park. All the journalists asked me what I'd come to Newcastle for. My reply? I've come to win the English championship. At the beginning, people were a little bit sceptical because there were really strong teams in the

Premiership – Manchester United, Liverpool, Blackburn and Arsenal were strongly fancied – but today it's not a question worth asking. Everyone knows how close we came to winning the title. I've got absolute confidence in the players and the management, and I'm proud to be a part of a club that is developing, building itself up into something great.

I spent the day in Newcastle before flying to France to organise my move to England. I would return, to start work as a fully fledged Magpie, seven days later. The Newcastle management offered me a week off, to take some holiday time to organise everything. Holiday time? Unfortunately, I had used it all up negotiating with Barcelona.

When I returned to France, everyone was perplexed that I had signed for Newcastle. It was a bolt out of the blue. The problem was that people didn't know much about the team, they thought the city was a dump, and considering all the other clubs that had expressed an interest, and knowing the way I play, and on the back of intense speculation that I was bound for Barcelona, it was a shock. I kept saying, 'Don't make judgements now, you have to look ahead.' Quite honestly, people are always asking questions about why people do things, but so what? That's life. Life is full of people analysing other people's motives. It didn't take long for people to understand. After reports filtered home about Newcastle's phenomenal start to the season, all those criticisms were consigned to the dustbin. They changed their tune: 'God, it's brilliant!' was the new chorus. The sort of things people asked before, like 'Why on earth did you pick Newcastle?' were no longer valid. I wouldn't say I was smug – I'm waiting to win the championship for that – but at least now everyone is backing me to the hilt in order that I might become a champion.

94

I first met my new team-mates at the training ground in Durham. I arrived and shook hands with everybody there. I think they thought it was a bit formal, but it's normal French politeness – there is nothing very strange about it. There were a lot of questions. Is he good, is he bad? That's to be expected with a new player, everyone is curious. My initial impression was that they were all very nice, but I knew they were still wondering whether I was a good player and a good guy.

I met Kevin Keegan for the first time. Some people find it amazing that I could sign for a club without ever meeting the manager, particularly after the problems I had with my previous coach. But I wasn't worried about it in the slightest. Everything about Newcastle had been so positive from the first minute they made contact with me, and in a haystack of optimism, why waste your energy looking for a needle of pessimism? As soon as I said hello to Kevin I knew any concern would have been totally misplaced. He was very friendly straightaway. He said some words in French to welcome me: 'Comment ça va?' and 'Allez les Verts!' He has an excellent memory as he was referring to St Etienne, who lost to Liverpool in the European Cup, when Keegan scored one of the goals in the second leg at Anfield. Keegan is very good to me when I play well and good to me when I don't play so well. He knows I have a lot of possibilities on the pitch. He always encourages me to show my best form on the pitch, and that's why I love him. Terry McDermott and Kevin Keegan are very good for one another. They are very important for the club because they are legends, they know their football, and they have such a reservoir of experience from their playing careers. It's great for Newcastle to have two men like this at the helm.

I was surprised to discover the training camp was so open. In Paris it was better – the facilities were private, only for us. In Newcastle, we train at Durham University. You can be playing head tennis and at one o'clock you get kicked off the court by four women who arrive saying they have booked the court to play badminton. So you have to stop your head tennis! That's the one bad thing I have encountered in terms of organisation at Newcastle. I have seen the plans for the new development they are proposing which looks fantastic. They say it's going to take about four years until completion. When I signed I remember them telling me, 'For next season, we'll have a new training camp.' But they haven't even started to lay the tarmac for the road that takes you to the site yet.

Aside from that pedantic point, I think it's the French clubs who need to learn from the English about how to run a football club. I have noticed a fundamental difference between the set-up of the clubs either side of the Channel. The basic problem in France is that you don't just have one supremo who is responsible for the club, the overseer, the man in control, like Sir John Hall in Newcastle. In France, a club's finances are pooled together from the town hall, the municipality and the region, so no one is actually prepared to run it correctly. It's too haphazard. When it's other people's money rather than your own investment, you don't have the same protectiveness and interest and care. It's all dribs and drabs of grants from different public bodies, therefore the running of the funding is incredibly inefficient. And open to abuse. You could say, perhaps euphemistically, accounting in French clubs isn't always straightforward. It wasn't only Marseille who hit trouble with the revenue services. Small clubs were often being run as if they were very profitable when in fact they were haemorrhaging finances. I saw this first-hand at Brest! They always, foolishly, try to live above their means – a champagne taste from a water pocket. They are Ordinary Joes wanting to live as if they were Kings.

In Newcastle, it's very nice to see something which is run in a healthy, uncomplicated way – scandal-free in other words! There is one force in command of the club, with a businesslike approach fit to match the passion for success. Sir John Hall is the main man for the future of Newcastle because he wants to build a magnificent club, and he has the resources and the drive to do it. He has a lot of ambition for the club, and he knows what it means to the people of Newcastle. He wants to make the club successful not only in England, but also in Europe. He wants to build something special in the North East. Also, he's a very nice man. He's very close to us.

French clubs generally aren't wealthy. In England there is so much more money going in and out of the clubs. More than anyone in French football could ever imagine. They spend a fortune on players, and massive income is generated from sponsorship and marketing. France could learn a lot from observing this. There is a real difference of mentality. What you can do in England is possible because there is a football culture to enable you to do it. For example, in Paris, nobody walks around the streets with a PSG shirt on, because people will look you up and down as if you have green hair or live in the toilet. In Newcastle you are bare without one! It's a sign that you belong. It's a perfectly normal thing to do. Obviously, this lifestyle means Newcastle can march down commercial roads that Paris can't, unless they find a way of setting a new trend.

It doesn't bother me that Newcastle paid £2.5 million for me, or £6 million for Les Ferdinand, or £3.5 million for David Batty. The financial price doesn't preoccupy me. They paid a reasonable price for me and I wouldn't have liked the club to have paid over the odds for me, or broken the bank. It's a lot of money, but it was probably the cheapest transfer of the close-season. I can't speak for all players, but I earn more money in Newcastle than I did in France. It's better for me.

I don't really think that English football has a lot to learn from the game in France, but I do think that English football has to get results in European football. Aside from that, everything in England is brilliant. Manchester United, Newcastle, Arsenal, Liverpool – all these clubs really impress me, they are superb.

People in Europe think English football is just push and run, but Newcastle, and Liverpool and Manchester United, don't play like that. Newcastle have a very attacking team because we have the players to play that way. It was important to me to play in a team with an attacking style. We try to build something by passing the ball, go forward when we can. It's not like the English football I saw on the TV a few years ago. I was pleasantly surprised to find this, and I'm very proud of the style of football Newcastle play. It's all down to Keegan and the mentality of the players. We want to play exciting football, and we want to have success playing this way. I remember Keegan said to me when I joined: 'You know David, we don't play the way everyone in France thinks we play. We don't play kick and run. We try to play football, especially in midfield.' Rob Lee, Peter Beardsley, David Batty, Faustino Asprilla and me, we try to play attractive, attacking football, and that's good for the English game. Maybe the preconceptions people in Europe have about English football – determined, strong in the head, kick and rush – are wrong: I think English football is changing.

CHAPTER ELEVEN

Vive la Différence
Long Live the Difference

Mad dogs and Englishmen
Go out in the midday sun,
The Japanese don't care to,
The Chinese wouldn't dare to,
Hindoos and Argentines sleep firmly from twelve to one
But Englishmen detest a siesta.

Noel Coward

My former team-mates in France always joke with me about the weather. I always reply, 'I didn't come here for the weather.' I have to live with it. If every day I wake up, look out the window, see it's miserable and say, 'Bloody hell it's horrible,' I would go mad! I take my life as it comes. When I call my friends it's a pleasure to speak in my language. Most of the time I think in French but speak in English, and at the end of the day it's very tiring. I want to be able to think in English too . . . We'll see. I've noticed the French are more likely to come up and be friendly to a foreigner, to try to converse in their language, but in England it's hard to find anyone who will say anything other than *'Bonjour'*.

You have to know English in the modern world, but I don't think the English make much effort with other languages. I didn't have much vocabulary when I arrived and, although I had a base of English in the back of my mind from school, I couldn't communicate exactly what I wanted to say to everyone, which was frustrating. But every day I improved, making sure I learned more words. Now I'm pretty good. I've learned more in one year living here than I could in seven years at school. Fortunately, since day one I have managed to understand everybody. Maybe all those years ogling at Madame Bonnemaine weren't wasted after all! I must confess she didn't speak in a Geordie accent. But it's the same in France, people from different parts of the country have a different dialect. My grandmother speaks Provençal and people in Paris don't understand her at all. I've picked up some Geordie because I hear it every day. Especially from people like Lee Clark, and they don't make them much more Geordie than him. It's very nice. I like it. Allreet. Way, aye man. Cheers mate!

The squad is full of different personalities. Some come from London, some from the Midlands, some from Newcastle, some from abroad. We all speak a different language! Well, the same language but different accents. It's a good mix. They are all very nice lads. Sometimes we all meet up in the city and go out for a night 'on the tiles' – it's a fantastic atmosphere. If you want to win something having a good camaraderie is essential. If you're playing well, it's not an issue because everyone is happy, but if you have a few bad results, the spirit of the team can pull you through. You can all support each other and bounce back. Say, 'Hey come on, we can do better.' Everyone is very focused on the football. I soon discovered every player was united in the belief that we could win the championship and qualify for the European Champions League. And that belief was infectious. I believed it too.

Most of the players were extremely welcoming to me. I lived in a hotel for the first few weeks until I found a house and they frequently came to see me and took me out into town, maybe to a pub for a couple of drinks. It was good because I was staying in the same hotel as Les Ferdinand and Warren Barton, who had both moved up from London. We would have a laugh over breakfast together. Sometimes we went to the cinema after training. That was a great help, because it prevents you from feeling lonely. My family didn't join me from Paris until after my first six weeks in Newcastle.

Mentally, I found the move tough. It happened so quickly and it was quite difficult to adapt to such rapid change. When I first went into town with Les and Warren, people would mob them for autographs and they ignored me because they didn't know me. That was an advantage because I was able to be very quiet and keep myself to myself, which I needed so I could have time to think about all the new things that were happening in my life. But it's not the same now . . .

I think it's important to live for the present and the future, but you don't have to forget everything that's happened in the past. I still follow the results from France. I look out for the results on television, I see some French games on TV and, of course, I take particular interest in the progress of PSG, and the French teams competing in Europe. It's great when you see your friends – those who had been alongside you only a few months before – playing on the pitch. I don't like reading the papers, but it's enough to find out the results and see if my friends play well. I speak to them quite a lot. We compare notes about our clubs, the games, the life, the weather, the fans, the mentality, the golf . . .

From what I had heard, all English footballers play a lot of golf, which I was delighted about. If I was going to be stranded on a desert island, and I could take only five things with me, it would be a big kitchen to cook all the fish, vegetables and fruit, a boat, my children, my wife and a golf bag. I have played golf with Seve Ballesteros and Jose-Maria Olazabal. I have even played with Kevin Keegan! The first time we played for fun, in the rain, and he beat me on the last hole. The next day we played for real, and I got my revenge to beat him by a convincing margin. Above all, I would love to meander around the 18 holes with one famous golfer in particular. I told Kevin, 'I would get so much pleasure to play a round with Sean Connery, because he's my idol.' I admire his charisma. When I arrived in Newcastle I was looking forward to a lot of opportunities to play golf. But we had a harsh winter and we couldn't play too much. By the time the weather had warmed up, we were focused on the championship and golf was the last thing on our minds.

In one respect, I prefer golf to football. If you make a mistake, you are on your own and you don't have the weight of guilt and responsibility that you have let down the other 10 men in the team. But football is about a union. It's very wrong if a player tries to blame another individual just to save his own skin. I always try to guard against that.

I found pre-season training difficult at first, because I had been out of action for a month and a half. I hadn't been doing anything except trying to organise my transfer. I didn't feel very fit, and pre-season was knackering. The rest of the squad had already been training for a week, which didn't help either. We worked very intensively for one month. Keegan told me: 'The first month is crucial for the rest of the season. We will train very hard in this month.' It wasn't easy for me, because I was out of shape thanks to my summer of inactivity. I had to work very hard to catch up in terms of fitness. Every day we went running in the forest, and after training I was exhausted. I slept a lot, in fact I couldn't have slept more if I had drunk a dozen bottles of Newkey Brown every day! In France it's different because you don't have such a long break. You have only 20 days away from the club. Now I know I have to work during my holiday if I want to be ready for the pre-season training. Otherwise I turn up three kilograms overweight and I feel it. I will have to do a pre-season pre-season!

Training sessions are longer in England. In France you have two sessions, one in the morning and one in the afternoon, but it is much more relaxed. Kevin Keegan has one session every day, but it is very intense. I wasn't used to keeping full concentration for three hours. It's a mix of ball work and physical work, but there is a lot of emphasis on the physical. I prefer working with the ball, which Kevin Keegan knows. We go in the gym, then out onto the pitch, then back in the gym, and then my achilles heel – half an hour running in the woods. I was 200 metres behind the rest of the group when I went for my first run in the forest. I was running on my own. Nothing like making a good impression! But I am always encouraged by the fact that Michel Platini, the greatest ever French footballer, didn't like training either. It didn't seem to do him any harm!

My first game in Newcastle colours was a pre-season friendly at Rushden and Diamonds. To run out onto the pitch in the black and white shirt was a great experience. I was proud to be the first French guy to be in Newcastle's team. It was the first time in four years that I had pulled on a new shirt – after the blue of PSG and France – and that was a stimulating feeling. I was really excited, buzzing to feel something other than the Paris shirt on my chest. Then we went to Scotland for a game in Edinburgh against Hearts, and then we played Celtic in Glasgow. With each game I felt better and better. I was getting fitter and adapting to my new life and to a new game of football. I wanted to adapt very quickly. I didn't find it a problem to play well on the pitch. I think if you have a bit of quality, you can adapt your football to whatever country or style you are playing.

I wasn't particularly surprised by English football. I knew plenty about what to expect. In France, we watch a lot of the other leagues, and thanks to the advances in satellite television I was familiar with the Italian, Spanish and English leagues. We get to feel the different flavours of the various championships, because football is broadcast from all over the place. The fact that Eric was playing in England meant we saw a lot of English football on TV. So it wasn't a great surprise to find a different style of football here. From what I had observed, I had an inkling of how to play football this side of the Channel. I expected it to be harder and faster than in France. You have to be very strong physically. There is no time to wait in the game here, to pause and find the best moment to make a killer pass or run. So often it is end-to-end. You don't have time to think, you just have to play. All the time, I am adjusting my game to adapt better to the English tempo. There is a different approach to football in every country throughout the world, that is the charm of the game. In England I have discovered another style of football and I intend to rise to the new challenges.

I try to push myself to perform well in every game, because when you buy a foreigner you expect and want more from him than an Englishman in England or a Frenchman in France. That's normal. Even if I might feel tired, I can't play at a leisurely pace. You can't stop for a moment. If you want to get results you have to give of your best all the time; you can't stop just because you feel like it. Kevin Keegan is very important in terms of motivating everyone in the team. It pleased me to find he encourages rather than provokes a response. He might say, 'Hey David, you have to play better because I know you can play better.' It's vital to have someone like this at the club. I was happy with the way I played in the first six months. After that it was harder. My priorities changed. My only thoughts were with winning the championship, not personal success.

I had to adapt to the English football routine off the pitch too. This has been a bonus. The atmosphere is always good in the coach coming back from a game, a very different routine to what I experienced in France. We have some fish and chips, some beers, *Only Fools and Horses* on the video! It's great, Rodney and Del Boy. At first I thought, 'Bloody hell, what is this?' because I didn't understand it. But now I think it's very good. I like Del Boy; I think he is very funny. We went to Bournemouth for three days just before we played Arsenal, and we went to Harry Ramsden's for fish and chips on the beach. It's the English life. When you live in England, you have to try what the English people do every day. I enjoy it to the full.

CHAPTER TWELVE

Affrontement Culturel
Culture Shock

*You really speak the most wonderful accent without
the slightest English.*

George Mikes, 'How to be an Alien'

On my first day in Newcastle, I went for a drive around
town with my wife and said, 'This is where we are
going to live.' I realised what an enormous step I had
taken when my wife started crying in my arms in the car.
I thought, 'Maybe this isn't going to be so easy.' She was
afraid of what life would be like and frightened of losing
our identity, the life we had constructed in Paris. When
you leave a life you love and are comfortable with, you
have no assurances about what you will find in its place.
It's natural to be apprehensive of how things might
develop. My biggest concern was how my family would
cope. It's no problem being a player, because you have
your own life with the club, and training and matches to
occupy you, mentally and physically, every day. But for the
ones who stay at home it's more difficult. I never had time

107

on my hands to feel lost or homesick.

You have to change your whole life when you move clubs. When you are alone it poses no problems. With my first moves I had no one to worry about but me, and when we were very young and we didn't have children it was easy. Now we have to consider Andrea's schooling and it's difficult for him. Changing country is really something – it's not a decision you take lightly to uproot and leave your family and friends. At the beginning, Coraline thought it was going to be really hard, but in life you can get used to anything. You get used to a new lifestyle, new friends. Life goes on and you forget all the fears you had. Setting up home in a new country is a big change, but it's not earth-shattering.

Newcastle is completely different from Paris. Paris is an amazing place, I can't say anything negative about it. It's so romantic. It took time for me to become aware of the difference in lifestyle, for me to crave the things I didn't have any more. I didn't miss anything about France at first. I didn't have time to, I was too busy discovering Newcastle: the football, my team-mates, the city. But after a couple of months I realised, 'I miss my friends, my family, my life in Paris, the South of France, the sea, my village . . .' It's no different from if an English person went to live in France and after a while they would think, 'I want to go back to my own country.' After a while, I appreciated what a life I had in Paris. But I tried not to wallow in that. I always try to be positive. If you want to live a new life to the full, it does you no good to think about your old life.

It was at this time that Kevin Keegan was very kind and understanding. He told me, 'David, if you want to go back to France for a few days to fix everything, it's not a problem. I know what you are going through. I know how difficult it can be moving to a new country because I felt it when I went to Hamburg. I had the same problems in adapting. When I was in Hamburg, staying in a hotel, I was very low because I missed a lot of things in England, especially my friends and family.'

I wear a chain with three charms around my neck: one is the crest of St Tropez where I was born, which bears the motto 'forever faithful'; one for Andrea, my son; and one a crafted dolphin, just to remind me of the feeling of being near the sea. It's symbolic; it keeps me in touch with the Mediterranean. Yes, there is the North Sea in Newcastle, but when I look at that sea I confess I feel nothing. Looking out to the ocean in the north-east of England, the view is dominated by oil refineries and offshore platforms. For me it's not a pretty sight. I love dolphins, I love the sea, I love the water. I think I was a dolphin in another life. At least I hope so.

When you are a foreigner, people aren't interested that you need to go home, recharge yourself. They pay a lot of money and they want results. Sometimes people forget that footballers are human beings. Keegan never forgets. He has had this experience and he knows what it is to be a foreigner and to have difficulties. It's good for me to have someone like Keegan here. He was a great player, he is a great manager, but, above all, he is a good lad. I honestly believe that is inherent to being a good manager. If you're not a good lad you can't be a good manager because you can't analyse and empathise with the different mentalities of your players. You have to be able to feel what makes the players tick, what they are thinking, how they contribute to the spirit of the club. A manager can't go around like a horse wearing blinkers. He has to open his eyes and look around.

Keegan is able to be on the same level as the lads, but also he is above – he must be – so he can see what is happening in the club. He genuinely knows when something happens, or when someone has a problem. He has a lot of experience himself to spot these things. Keegan is crucial to the club. I have had a lot of managers in my life, and Keegan and Artur Jorge, my coach at Matra Racing and PSG, have been the most influential. Jorge wasn't as friendly with the players as Keegan is, for he kept himself more at a distance. Both these men are very straight and very honest. An honest football manager can't be loved by everyone. In general, if a player is picked, he loves the manager; if he isn't, he doesn't love his boss. That is the life of a manager. But Keegan is loved by everybody. He has a different approach, kind to everyone, even if they don't satisfy his ideals.

Whenever I felt unsettled, I reminded myself that I didn't choose to come to Newcastle for the town, I came for the football and the club and the people who are so incredibly involved – 100 per cent committed to the club. I was instantly amazed by the warmth of the fans and the good vibes that hung in the air wherever I went – you don't find anything like that at any club in France.

Here I just have a simple family life. I don't get up to all that much outside of football because I am concentrating on my game, that's all. I'm a foreigner now. And I now know what it means to be a foreigner in the team. At Paris Saint-Germain, the Brazilian Rai played for us. Not a lot of people spoke to him or spent much time with him. I understand now what he must have felt because it's the same for me now. But I don't need to have a lot of friends and to be invited out all the time. I don't ask for the players to be my friends. We all get on very well, but I don't feel the need to have bosom buddies. Everyone feels what they want to feel. We just meet up when we decide to go out. We are neighbours with Warren Barton and his wife, Candy, who speaks a little bit of French. I just want to have a quiet life and be content and have a positive atmosphere with everyone.

Sometimes I come back from training and I think, 'What am I going to do with myself this afternoon?' That's natural when you are in foreign climes. We take a drive, go to the seaside, go to Metroland. In Paris, you've got thousands of pursuits to follow – the Louvre, the Musée d'Orsay, Versailles, the museums, the parks, the boutiques, concerts . . . There are probably things to do here but I haven't yet discovered them. There's theatre and cinema, but it's all in English so it's hard work to understand it and it's impossible for my family. I took my son to see *Jumanji*, with Robin Williams, but he was pretty confused. He wanted to see it but he didn't understand a word. It's easier to live in Paris than Newcastle as a star. You can blend with the crowd. People in Paris don't only have football and you're not the only attraction around. In Newcastle there is Jimmy Nail and Sting, but they don't live in Newcastle. At the beginning of the season everything is new, everything is exciting, everything is beautiful. But the ambience alters when you have been there a few months. I don't want to be negative because if that's the way you feel you shouldn't live abroad.

It was very strange being an exiled Frenchman when our government embarked upon a nuclear testing programme. There was a lot of bad feeling all over the world, including in England. I wasn't proud about the tests, because I would prefer to have a free world. No nuclear armaments, no weapons, no guns. But so many countries have a nuclear bomb and they carry out tests. France needed to be ready like all the other countries and it's very difficult when everybody has nuclear weapons to turn your back on it. It became a scandal, but it was something we had to do. The outcry in the rest of the world was hypocritical because some nations benefited from French experiments. At least now it's finished. Hopefully we will have no more nuclear bombs in the world.

Even though England and France are only a Channel apart, there are many cultural differences to adapt to. Food is a utilitarian thing in England, there is less of the joy of eating. Food has to be a pleasure in France, particularly in my region. There is an old Provençal proverb which says, 'There's no such thing as a pretty good omelette.' In other words it can only be very good or very bad. My friends from the South of France think it must be hard to stomach living in England because of the cuisine. I don't agree, because I like trying something different and trying to get used to it. It was never my intention to go to England and live like a Frenchman. The only thing I really miss is baby artichokes, a Provençal speciality. Part of the appeal and enriching experience of living abroad is to throw yourself into local life. To see these differences is interesting, fulfilling. I want to eat what the English eat every day. I want to go to the places they go. When I go back to my country, I tell my friends how they live. It's part of my general knowledge and cultural awareness. But I can't deny it has made me appreciate French food even more! The only thing I don't understand is why some English food has sugar and salt in the same dish. To my palate it's disgusting.

When I first wanted to have a cigarette, I asked the team, 'Does anyone object if I smoke a cigarette?' I was amazed by the look on their faces. They were horrified. I don't think many players smoke in English football. In Paris, maybe six or seven players from the team smoke. But it's like everything, you mustn't abuse your body. I don't like drinking that much. We don't drink a lot in France, and we don't drink the same things. We don't drink a lot of beer. In England I have found some beer specialists in the team. I had never seen brown ale before I came to Newcastle. In France we drink more spirits and wine. Drinking just for the sake of it is not my thing. Just drink, drink, drink . . . it's not necessary. You can have a good party without it. When I go out, I know my limit and I never go past it. I have had this experience in the past and I didn't like it. If I feel that I can't drive my car, and so I won't be able to get myself home, I stop myself and say, 'Hey David, come on, you can't do that.' It's very funny when I see people who drink so much they fall over or they vomit. It's in the mentality here. In France people occasionally drink a lot in terms of quantity, but you don't see people rolling around drunk. In England, as soon as the pubs shut, people are looning around dizzily.

I have noticed that the women who idolise me in England behave differently to my female fans in France. In England they really touch you; they are really brazen, all touching and pawing and suggestive. Maybe French women think the same thing, but they are much more subtle about it. They just look you up and down in a provocative but more cool and reserved way. The touching doesn't bother me – well, I suppose it does depend where they touch me! Also English women drink. I get the impression that women in England are pretty independent and self-sufficient. For example, in England you get groups of women going out together, they have their own evenings doing women-only things. They go to the pub together and, if they fancy a bloke, well, off they go! That is something that really struck me. In France, you won't see women acting so openly. They worry too much about what people think.

When I go out with my wife in England, the women don't come up to me. When I go out without her they come, but if you open the door everyone comes in, so I don't walk around like that too much. I try to avoid it. I don't go around asking for it. I must say I don't go out that much alone, and that is one of the reasons! But when I do go out, although it seems a bit pretentious to say it, I could get any old girl. It's so easy, but as that's the way it is you have to be careful what impression you're giving. At the end of the day you have to know what you want. But it isn't necessarily that easy to live like that.

If my daughter Carla brought home a footballer one day, I would have one piece of advice for her. She should always keep both eyes open, and even when she is asleep, she should keep one eye open!

When I arrived in England everyone was obsessed with the reputation of the French Romeo. I know plenty of Englishmen who are equally as sentimental as Frenchmen. Maybe he goes about it in a slightly less romantic way, but that's only because of cultural differences. Stereotypes are strange – if an Englishman or a Frenchman likes women, it's exactly the same thing.

I am macho as well, very Italian. A case of 'You stay in the kitchen and I go out.' It's bad, I know, but it's the Italian mentality for you. Meander into a southern European restaurant and the men will be sitting around doing nothing but chatting and laughing and keeping themselves amused while the women do all the work. This is a typical Mediterranean situation. I love the Italian mentality. Especially the traits passed through generations of countryfolk, rather than the people who come from the big cities. I like tradition and in Italy there is tradition in abundance. The younger generation are more into fashion, and there is nothing wrong with the influence of something superficial like fashion, but it's no bad thing to keep a place in the corner of your head reserved for history and principles.

The French have a very outdated stereotype of Englishness, seeing it as a sort of superior Lord Haw-Haw type. It's kind of weird, but it stems from a famous film in France called *La Grande Vadrouille*, 'The Great Jaunt', which was set among the army during the War. The

114

English characters all sit around having cups of tea, speaking with plums in their mouths, mid-battle! It's very funny, but in fact it's a very affectionate image, not at all aggressive. Myself, I find that the English are macho too, albeit in perhaps a different way from the Italians.

CHAPTER THIRTEEN

Le Grand Huit
Rollercoaster

Il s'appelle David,
Il est un seulement breed,
Très rapide, un génie.
Il est une artiste, qui peindre avec son pieds.
Il est 'superbe', 'magnifique', 'un Geordie'.
Notre David.
He is called David,
He is a sole breed,
Very fast, a genius.
He is an artist, who paints with his feet.
He is super, magnificent, a Geordie.
Wor David.

> Newcastle fan Adam Dallinger,
> 'Ode to David Ginola'

It is 19 August 1995. I was about to reap the rewards of all those gruelling miles dribbling past the trees. Coventry City were the visitors for my Newcastle debut, my St James' Park debut, my Premier League debut. I was full of apprehension. This was where my English adventure really began. I had the wide open road in front of me and I had no idea where my journey would take me. I emerged through the tunnel to see St James' Park full of 36,000 gregarious Geordies for the first time. It was a stirring sight. My pulse quickened. I wanted to give my best. We won 3–0 on a blazing afternoon and the experience of the game felt tremendous. All the press were buzzing afterwards, the post-match mood was brilliant. It was a brand-new scene and I was thrilled with what I found. After the first game people were complimentary: 'Ginola is brilliant, a very good signing, one of the best wingers around.' Very positive things. I smiled to myself. You've made a good choice here, David.

Our first away game was against newly promoted Bolton. I have heard it said that there are no easy games in the Premiership, and the leaders can always have trouble beating a team at the bottom of the league. Every championship has the same problem, while one team strives to win the league the other scrambles to stay in it. It's not the same battle, but when the two adversaries enter the arena, both have much to fight for. Different thinking but the same goal. It's really a question of what is going on in the players' heads. In England they have a very strong will and if you're up against a team who has this will to win it's going to be a Herculean match even if they aren't particularly good. An English team will really dig in and say, 'We're not going to go down. We will not give up without a fight.' Defiance is a very English trait. In France players are more likely to think, 'Well what can we do? We're as good as down.' They almost willingly concede the game before they have stepped foot on the pitch.

I scored my first Newcastle goal at Hillsborough in our third league game at Sheffield Wednesday. It was even more gratifying because it was televised in France and I

The start of a new life in Newcastle. (*Popperfoto*)

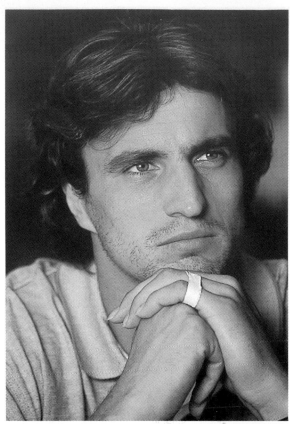

Ginola in thoughtful mood: time for a new challenge? Or a game of golf with his father, perhaps? (*Chris Cole/Allsport* and *Temp Sport/Colorsport*)

Burning with ambition against the awesome AC Milan, and Marcel Desailly of France, in the European Cup in April 1995. (*Sipa/Colorsport*)

Ginola's best game for France, against Israel in October 1993. Eric Cantona is in support. (*Sipa/Colorsport*)

And his worst. Coming on for Papin against Bulgaria. Gérard Houllier, the manager of the national side, described Ginola as a 'criminal' for his performance in the game. (*Sipa/Colorsport*)

Down to business. (*Action Images*)

The turning point, March 1996. Unable to stave off Manchester United at St James' Park. (*Colorsport*)

Magic moments at Anfield. Ginola celebrates with Tino Asprilla after he has scored the goal that put Newcastle 2–1 up. But it wasn't enough. (*Colorsport*)

An unbelievable season. (*Action Images*)

Thumbs up. (*Action Images*)

knew my family were watching, not to mention all those who were sceptical about my decision to join Newcastle. I remember the response of the Newcastle players after I scored. They all ran over to congratulate me; I felt taller than my six feet. When you are a foreigner you know you must produce a good performance all the time, so I was delighted to get off the mark so quickly. The best thing about playing at Sheffield Wednesday was to see Chris Waddle, or Chris 'Magic' Waddle as was his full moniker in France. I had played against him when I was with PSG and he was at Marseille. It was a beautiful day in Sheffield and there was a huge burning sun in the sky – I thought for one moment I was in the Velodrome Stadium in Marseille! Waddle was my hero when I was in the South of France – he was everybody's hero. If you ask anyone in the South of France what they think of Chris Waddle they will all smile: 'Magic'. I used to watch him on the television and every game, I would come up with the same adjective. He was arguably the most popular player in the French league during his three years with Marseille. When I arrived in England, Chris had predicted in one of the newspapers that if I played as well as I am capable, I would be as popular as one of the boys from Take That!

I couldn't have had a better start to a new championship. Our next game was just down the road against neighbours Middlesbrough. There was a lot of praise after that game which gave me an extra boost of confidence. I showed a few tricks on the edge of our own box, bamboozling their full back Neil Cox, to get the ball out of defence and into attack, and it was analysed again and again on the television, then I found space for a cross from which Les Ferdinand powered in a header to score the only goal of the game. I was thoroughly enjoying my football.

The partnership between Les and me created a barrage

of goals at the beginning of the season. He is a fantastic player, especially in the air. For a striker to get on the end of a cross is all a question of timing. He scored so many goals because he was intuitively in the right place at the right time. For me to cross the ball to him was easy, it was something I did all the time for George Weah in Paris. However the funny thing is, my left foot is not my natural foot, but for five years I played on the left-hand side of midfield and attack, so I had to work hard to deliver an equally good ball with my weaker foot. I had to apply myself hard and now I can reap the benefit. With Keith Gillespie on the other wing we had an effective balance. He played brilliantly until he was injured, and then we had to reorganise our tactics. That made it more difficult for me because the opposition concentrated their efforts on my wing.

I won the award for Player of the Month after the opening weeks of the championship. Everything was perfect for me. The way that you play in your first few games in a new country is crucial. You need to show people what you can do immediately, otherwise the pressure mounts and it becomes a monumental test to prove that you are a good player. People want to pigeon-hole you: 'Oh, this player, he's a real handful, that player, he's useless . . .' Everyone does it and once you have been put neatly into a compartment, you need to be Houdini to get out. I am fully aware my form dipped after Christmas, but at least people know what I am capable of, and I am positive I will get back to my peak. If it had been the other way round, and I was off-key in the first half of the season and then Player of the Month after Christmas, the jury would still be out on David Ginola.

I knew the importance of making a good impression and, fortunately, the start of the season was wonderful. From day one people were supportive and positive. It certainly helps to erase the nerves you have in a new environment.

It's like starting a new job or a new school. For the first few weeks you try to do the right thing, try to please everyone until you are sure you fit in. Then you can relax and be yourself. The fact that the team were playing with so much confidence and there was such a buoyant spirit made it easier for me. They helped me to ride on the crest of a North Sea wave. We went from strength to strength. We topped the league from the first day of the season and we lost only one game in our first 20 and won every league game at home until March. Some of the newspaper headlines claimed we were invincible. Newcastle were a different class, mate.

I didn't want it to go to my head. I was delighted to have made a promising start to my first season in England, but I had to check myself to make sure I didn't get carried away. As a professional footballer, I don't think one has the right to show everyone what a good footballer you are only to enable you to rest on your laurels. I wanted to maintain that level of performance.

I began to feel the pace after Christmas. It was the first time I had played through the winter without having a break. After ten years, this was the first time I had experienced a change in the rhythm of the season. In England there are three matches over the holiday period, but I was used to a two-week break, which is warmly welcomed every winter by the players in France. It's beneficial as a mental rest as much as a physical one. We were thankful for some much-needed respite. We could take a holiday, spend some quality time with our families. I usually went skiing. Of course I had to be careful to guard against injury, but I am a very confident skier, I know what I'm doing. The English think it's all right to steamroller straight through the season, but they don't know any better! There has been a lot of debate about having a winter break in England. The players are in

121

favour. We spoke about it in the Newcastle dressing room and the players agreed a break would be a good move. I understand that Christmas and New Year matches are as traditional as turkey and hangovers, but I'm sure the quality of the football over the whole season would improve if we had a break at some stage. It would mean we wouldn't get such a long holiday during the summer, especially when there is a major tournament such as the World Cup or the European Championship, but having a rest half way through the season certainly compensates.

When I first arrived in Newcastle, there was a lot of comment suggesting I wouldn't be the same player in winter. They predicted that, because I come from the south and the sun, I would fall apart with the ice and the snow. I thought it was a funny thing to say. It amused me. But, to a degree, it was true. When the snow arrived it wasn't the best thing for my football. The climate has an effect on my football. If I get out onto the pitch and it resembles an ice rink, I have to confess I don't play the same. I can't feel what I'm doing properly. I am a player who needs to be able to feel the ground in order to express myself with the ball. For a defender, the state of the ground is not so vital, because his job is to take the ball. But the job of an attacker is to play with the ball and create something with it. It's as if the attacker is trying to draw some art on the pitch and the defender is trying to erase it. Having a feel of the surface is fundamental. It's easier to paint on an absorbent texture like canvas than a slippery one like foil. Snow is not ideal for my football, but I suppose, it's just another thing for me to get used to.

The sun is my inspiration. There are people from sunny climes who find England extremely depressing. There are days when I do get up and the sun shines and the day begins better, but there are other days when you get up to see that grey low hanging cloud, it's very depressing. It's really sad. At eight o'clock in the morning your inspiration is all used up!

After the wave of optimism that soared over the first half of the campaign, I hit choppy waters in the New Year. The first real setback I encountered as an adopted Geordie was defeat by Chelsea in the FA Cup third round. I was excited to play in the FA Cup because of the tradition it carries all over the world. Every year, the final would be televised at three o'clock on a Saturday afternoon at Wembley and I eagerly watched the games in France. We were seconds away from going out at Stamford Bridge, but then . . . We felt the joy of a last-gasp goal as Les Ferdinand equalised in the 93rd minute. Chelsea won the replay, after, believe it or not, a last-minute goal from Ruud Gullit forced the game into extra time and then a penalty shoot-out. It was the first match we lost at fortress St James' Park. I don't subscribe to the opinion that you don't really lose when you go out on penalties. It was Chelsea who progressed, not Newcastle. In my eyes, it was without question a defeat. It was a pity. I think we had a great chance of beating Chelsea and if we had gone on from there, maybe we would have played our great rivals Manchester United in the semi-finals instead of them . . . After Chelsea knocked us out of the FA Cup, Sir John Hall tried to mask his disappointment by looking on the bright side. 'I want to win the league this season,' he said. At this time we were 10 points clear. 'Don't worry about that,' I replied.

In between the two Chelsea matches came the turbulent turning point for David Ginola's season. I arrived at a critical crossroads against Arsenal. This is the tale of the fiendish full-backs, the falling Frenchman, the repressive referee and the enraged elbow.

There had been a lot of nonsense written about my diving. It became a big deal to the extent that whenever I was fouled, I was booed and accused of cheating by opposition fans. This made me realise, for the first time, what it means to be a foreigner in a team. When you arrive in a new country, at first people can't say enough good things about you. The fans, the press, the players, everyone heaps praise onto your shoulders. For them, you are something intriguing – they have hopes, expectations and curiosity. These are positive states of mind. But there has to come a time when that changes. They are going to find something negative. In my case, they came up with this story about how I took dives all the time.

It all started after a Coca-Cola Cup match at Stoke when the manager Lou Macari accused me of diving to get their defender Ian Clarkson sent off. I have never tried to get another player sent off in my career. That's not within the spirit of football. I'm far more interested in playing the game. Anyway, it wasn't me who gave the defender a red card!

The Coca-Cola Cup game against Arsenal was where it all came to a head. During the match I honestly felt everything was going against me. It was a highly charged, competitive game and I was being fouled constantly. The Arsenal defender Lee Dixon continually clattered into me, at one time tackling straight through my shin. Then Nigel Winterburn tripped me just outside the penalty area, in the middle of a run from midfield into the box. I was shown a yellow card. I thought: 'What the hell is going on here? This is not possible. How can I play like this? The defender is beating the hell out of me and I'm the one who is getting the blame? The referee must be crazy!' It was beyond my comprehension. Anyway, why would I dive if I was in a scoring position?

I was getting more and more frustrated. I admit I stuck out an arm. It wasn't retaliatory or vindictive. I didn't lose my mind. Lee Dixon clasped my shirt and I just wanted to shrug him off so I was free to move. I never tried to elbow him. I never tried to connect with his head. I would do the same again in a replica situation. I would try to get free of someone who was tugging me back, and preventing me from playing football. I am on the pitch to play the game not to tussle with an opponent. I insist, I never intended to hit him. The referee showed me the red card and having to leave the field, surrounded by a barrage of noise, was a desperate feeling.

I felt like anyone would feel who is the victim of injustice. It's a horrible feeling. You are being victimised and you simply can't react to your aggressor. I felt very angry towards the referee. It would be simple if all I had to do was get hold of the referee and swipe him one, but you are not in a position to do that, however strong the urge might be. Well, physically you could do it, but spiritually you know that is an impossible scenario. If you do that, you're finished as a footballer. We haven't got the right to do that. We have to respect the rules of the game and the man who has to enforce them. But at the same time, the referee has to have integrity in order to command that respect. He can't carry any preconceived ideas about who he wants to win or what he thinks of an individual player on the field. He has to judge everyone on their merits in each particular game. That's why I thought what was going on here was very wrong. This was a match we could easily have won. It should have been going in our favour. Nigel Winterburn should have been sent off for a tackle from behind on Steve Watson, yet he was shown only a yellow card. And there was me, who had been trying to play football, shouldering all the blame and a red card to boot. Walking alone down the tunnel while the game was going on behind me was deeply depressing.

The only thing I learned from being sent off was the

meaning of unfairness. I have no problems with Lee Dixon. He was doing his job. In the end, he won the game and he won the private battle with me because I was dismissed.

Kevin Keegan and Terry McDermott were very worried. I got a lot of backing from people. Managers, players and fans were outraged, saying it was scandalous. 'The referee isn't letting him play football,' argued my supporters. Everyone was on my side, they thought it was crazy. At least people realise there are limits.

In football you have to learn to accept injustice from time to time, but that doesn't mean it's easy to take when it happens to you or your team. Nobody can embrace injustice – it's impossible. The problem is that referees are fallible because they are human beings and every human being has their own sensibility and their own preferences. It's human nature – we all prefer some things to others. For example, a referee who has always supported a team may find himself in the situation where he has to officiate in a game involving that team, and no matter how impartial he tries to be, there may be a moment where his personal preferences will get the better of his judgement. It might even be subconscious, but it might just happen he will blow his whistle when he should have kept silent.

The referee who sent me off didn't let me play football. I need the possibility to express myself and not to hear the whistle blown every single time I go near the ball. I don't expect to be let off if I do something wrong, but the ref should allow the game to flow, otherwise what do people come to football matches for? A football fan comes to the stadium to see the attackers attack, and the defenders tackling, in the true sense of the word. I have often come across referees who seem to favour the defence, and obviously the game is then deprived of the spectacular. Sometimes a trainer will tell his players to go in hard, to stop the talented players in their tracks because they are the most dangerous players. It is considered to be a legitimate tactic by some managers. I have seen too many murderous tackles to mention. If I come to see a football match, I want to see a spectacle, and I think I'm one of the players who can provide a spectacle. The referee is, above all, a judge on the football pitch, but he should encourage those eye-catching, sensational moments which make the crowd gasp, and if there is a player who uses force to prevent such thrills, the referee's job is to have a word with him. Tell him where to get off.

I don't believe the entertainers should get preferential treatment just because they might be more skilful than the next player, but everyone should be treated equally. That isn't always the case. As the saying goes, some are more equal than others. You can understand why Eric Cantona did what he did at Selhurst Park, because he was obviously burning with rage about the scenes that were going on around him. Eric lives his life according to his own rules. He is untameable. I cannot say that I would do the same. I wasn't in his position at that time. I understand perfectly well that you could feel like doing something like that, but the difference between feeling like doing it and actually doing it is enormous. When you are a professional you have a certain code of behaviour you have to respect, a certain duty to the profession. When Eric went into the crowd there was a kid practically in his line of fire and I think that kid must have suffered as a result.

After the incident at Selhurst Park, the French journalists rubbed their hands together with glee. When something like that happens with someone well known, they think, 'Great, tomorrow we're going to sell a lot of papers.'

I was very impulsive and occasionally temperamental when I was a young player. When you are 20 years old you take everything to heart but as you get older and you take a few knocks, you become a bit more philosophical about things. You try not to let things get to you, try to smooth the corners. Before, I used to shout and scream, go crazy about the ref. I'd never let go of things that bothered me, they clung to me like a leech. It almost got to the point of being obsessive. I simply couldn't let it lie. That was my character, but as I got older, people said to me, 'Come on David, you've got to cool down, be a bit calmer if you want to carry on playing.' It was a gradual process. I simmered down, tried not to fly into a rage so easily. I managed to turn a blind eye to provocation. Whatever people might say, against Arsenal I didn't return to my old ways and succumb to the red mist. It was an instinctive reaction to someone holding me back.

I was unlucky. I was banned for three games, and although that can sometimes be all over in 10 days, because of the way the games fell, I missed a month and a half. Unbelievable. Six weeks without a game! While a two-week rest in the middle of the season can be beneficial, six weeks when the rest of the team is in action cannot help.

I went back to France for a week to have a rest, to see my friends and family and get away from it all. I left the bleak grey and biting cold of the English winter, when it's dark when you wake up and night time again by five o'clock in the afternoon. I felt the contrast as soon as I stepped from the plane. February in the South of France is one of the most beautiful times of the year. The sun begins to glow again and the atmosphere is bright and uplifting. It's the carnival season. It's the time for the famous *Mardi Gras*, which literally means 'Fat Tuesday'. It originates from when people had a feast to celebrate the start of Lent. The tradition of the carnival is that the world is turned upside down. Historically, the lords of the manor and the minions would swap places for the day. Although I

128

didn't want the world turned on its head, I wouldn't have minded if my red card was rescinded. In Nice there is an annual festival and everyone comes onto the streets to admire the colourful floats. You can lose yourself in a world of imagination. It was the perfect escapism for me.

I came back to Newcastle and trained very hard to stay in peak shape. But it was a grind. For me to train every day for six weeks with no competitive edge was dispiriting. It was the first time in my life I had to endure such an experience. I had never been injured for such a long time, and I had never been suspended for such a long time. The football authorities didn't ban me for three games, they banned me for one and a half months. They know now that was a mistake. But it was too late, for me and the team. I couldn't recover all my sensations and feelings on the pitch. I lost everything.

Having six weeks with no game was a massive problem for me, and I never really regained my rhythm after such a long, enforced absence. I felt like someone killed me in my mind. It's like when someone runs the marathon, the same rhythm all the time, you click into pace at the end to go to win it, and someone in the crowd sticks out a foot and trips you. That's it. Finished. You can't recover. It's impossible.

When you are a competitor, all you want is to play every game. To see all your friends go off to a match while you stay behind is dreadful. That's no fun. Worst of all, you know you are absolutely fit. If you're injured you can't complain as you need treatment. But if you are in peak condition, that's another story.

When the lads were preparing for a game and I was just training, it was terrible. I couldn't get my head around the fact that my job was just to come and train. That's not me. I train just to be fit so that I can play games. It's a means to an end. But if you spend all week training and you have no game come Saturday, your mind has lost some important impetus. Playing football had been my life for 10 years. If having a long spell away from playing was a regular part of football, I would have known what to expect. But it was a new experience for me. I don't want that one again.

I was in France when we played West Ham at Upton Park. I felt very down when I heard the result: West Ham 2 Newcastle 0. It was a nasty surprise because I really thought the team would win at West Ham. It was churlish to think we had the title sewn up – I don't believe you can think that with 13 games to go, and so many hard games at that: Arsenal, Liverpool, Blackburn, Aston Villa . . . If I'm honest, I think we all thought we had done it when we were 12 points clear. The newspapers and television pundits said the race was over, the fans echoed the sentiments. And we believed it. Everybody believed it, not only in Newcastle but the whole of England. You could ask the opinion of any manager, player and fan from all the other teams in the league and they would give a unanimous response. Who is going to win the title? 'Newcastle, no question about that.' What was so incredible was that absolutely everyone sounded 110 per cent positive. Second place seems like failure set against so much heady expectation.

Even though we lost at West Ham, it wasn't really the beginning of our problems. Losing an away game isn't the end of the world, you can have a positive reaction, play at home the next game and get back to winning ways. But the title is often decided by how the top clubs perform away from home. In general, if you are top of the league and going for the championship, the crunch games take place away. You expect to win regularly at home – as we did – and even though we lost once at St James' Park against Man United, one defeat is reasonable. When I won

130

the league with Paris Saint-Germain, we played well at home but we were never in trouble away. Never. If we didn't take all three points we took one. We only lost one or two games away all season.

Newcastle's travelling record was to prove our undoing. We missed too many chances away, losing far too many games – Southampton, Chelsea, Manchester United, West Ham, Arsenal, Liverpool, Blackburn – it's too many to pretend to win the title. When we were 12 points clear, I was confident everything would be OK. In my head, I couldn't imagine we would lose too many games. We can't say we let ourselves down at home. But if we want to win the title next time we definitely have to pick up more points away. More than we did this season.

I went to the game against Middlesbrough at St James' Park, as a commentator for French TV. The game signalled the arrival of Faustino Asprilla. When he first signed I thought, 'Do we really need another player?' The team was playing well and we weren't in trouble. I knew he was an exciting player because I had seen him before on TV playing for Parma and Colombia. It's our job as players in a team to be a close-knit, compact group and we welcomed him. Anyway, he soon won us over because he's a good lad. He certainly made an impact in this game, coming off the bench to create the equaliser with his trickery. Some players say they find it very hard to watch a game from the sidelines. That wasn't too bad for me because we won. That's everything I wanted. It's not a problem for me to watch us collect three points. Thanks lads!

CHAPTER FOURTEEN

Une Minute
One Minute

Les Anglais ignorent quand ils sont battus
'The English don't know when they're beaten'

Napoleon

I was itching to get back into the team. My first game back, a 3–3 draw at Manchester City, was a display of everything that is great about the English game. It was frantically fast, compelling action, two attacking teams aching for a win, and an incredible comeback thrown in for good measure. We went 1–0 down then equalised, 2–1 down then equalised, 3–2 down and fought back again. Philippe Albert played a brilliant game. I tried so hard. I was so desperate to play, I wanted to give everything immediately. But you can't do it all in the first 20 minutes. We were pleased with the result, and the comeback, but the only problem was, while we were inconsistent, Manchester United were winning all their games, home and away. It was the opposite of the beginning of the season, when we strolled to a string of

133

victories while Manchester United stuttered.

I believe the crux of the championship was the Newcastle v Manchester United clash at St James' Park. The game was billed as a potential 'championship decider' in the pre-match hype. The pundits believed that the Reds had to win in order to stay in the race. If we won, the gap between us would have widened to a point where it was inconceivable they could catch us up. To add extra spice to the occasion, there was plenty of pontificating about the psychological effects the game could inflict on the winners and losers.

Of all the teams to lose to for our only home defeat in the league ... It was especially annoying after a fine performance in the first half, when we should have taken the lead. We dominated possession, made clear chances, but we couldn't find the net. Late in the game, they had one chance and scored. That's football. Our defence has been criticised during the campaign, but in this game the problem was we couldn't score. You can lose to Man United at Old Trafford but you have to win at home. The game was over, but it was worth more than three points to them. Maybe the psychologists had a point.

If you play badly and lose, somehow it's easier to get over. You can accept you didn't deserve anything. But when you play well and end up with nothing, it's very punishing. We played such good football against Man United, so it was difficult when afterwards we had to sit and analyse why we were beaten. There are no answers. I still can't explain why we lost this game. It can become a problem which nags away in your mind. Why did we lose? Why Manchester United? Why couldn't we get just one goal? We did everything. We didn't score, they scored. It was depressing. The first time we lost at St James' Park! It felt like something had broken. That can be psychologically damaging in the middle of a challenge where consistency is vital. This game was the key to the championship, and it unlocked the door for Manchester United.

The great strength of the squad is our ability to bounce back quickly. We don't mope around for too long. We are professional and it's our job to lift ourselves for the next game. OK, we were disappointed to be beaten but we had to pull it together to win the next game. We did exactly that, a convincing 3–0 victory over West Ham.

Manchester United and West Ham at home, Arsenal and Liverpool away: what a run! Just what you need at the crucial stage of the title race, huh? No sooner had we recovered from losing at home to Man United than we had to go straight down to London to play at Highbury, not our luckiest ground. After Christmas, trouble seemed to follow us whenever we left the sanctuary of St James' Park. It couldn't penetrate through the gates of our home, but it waited outside and always joined us when we boarded the coach and hit the motorway.

We lost 2–0, an appalling game for us. We were knocked off top spot for the first time in the season. Our fans always sang, 'We are top of the league, say we are top of the league!' at all our matches. Ominously, they didn't sing it during our game against Arsenal. That is when we knew we had been knocked from our perch. It was tough to stomach, the Toon Army had chanted that song at every match from October to March. The media dug their claws in and started to bite, 'All the pressure is on Kevin Keegan now . . .' Football is the number one preoccupation in England and facing a hyper press pack is to be expected. The race for the title is big news. Everyone had been talking about it for six months. That's a hell of a race. But the journalists began to talk about the pressure that was clamping down on Newcastle for the first time.

There was a different mood after that defeat, as we

played badly, so afterwards you just have to shake hands with the opposition and say thank you very much, well done. To pick ourselves up wasn't easy. It was like being strapped into an emotional roller-coaster. Plunging down a terrifying drop against Man United, mounting the heights again against West Ham, then another savage descent at Arsenal, and we had to creep back up, apprehensive about which direction we would hurtle in next. We were mentally, rather than physically, bruised. Regaining confidence was harder than recovering from the physical exertions of the match. It was a contrast to the previous defeat. We didn't do ourselves justice, so we couldn't feel sorry for ourselves.

But neither of those losses prepared us for the match against Liverpool, subsequently dubbed the 'game of the decade'. It was an awe-inspiring occasion. It was a meeting of two teams who want to play football with style and panache and speed. Together we created a compelling spectacle. I heard they sold the video of this game all over the world, for £10 million. All the countries that saw this game were so enamoured they wanted to buy the tape.

We had the chance to beat Liverpool three times in one season. There was quite a lot of media speculation about that, as no other team had done it before and we had an opportunity, having already beaten them in the league at home and in the Coca-Cola Cup at Anfield. At St James' Park, we didn't deserve to win the game. They played better than us but we won 1–0, in the last minute believe it or not. But that was the first part of the championship, when we had fortune shining on our side. What a poignant contrast with our form in the second half of the season.

We went 1–0 down very quickly. Les equalised, then I scored to make it 2–1. All the players thought that was a turning point. We were playing well, we had come back into the game and we were ahead. Now luck was surely with us. The team spirit was fantastic. I was really happy to score at Anfield, but the most important thing was that we were back in front. When you score goals and you win, it is always memorable. But when you score and you lose it never means much. The Liverpool players were unflustered. It went to 2–2 and then Tino scored a fantastic goal to put us back in front. Leading 3–2 with ten minutes to go, playing brilliant football, I really thought we had done enough. On top with just a few minutes remaining, I felt good. We were confident we could complete our hat-trick against Liverpool – home, away and in the League Cup – and then . . . Shock. Two late goals hit us like a slap on either cheek. Another three points slipped through our fingers as sand seeps through a timer. For a team who wants to be champions, that's just not good enough. It felt like all the rain in the whole world was falling onto our heads. The game finished and I thought, 'This is impossible, crazy. Losing a game like this is beyond imagination!' We tried everything, we gave everything.

It was the first time in the season any team had scored three goals at Anfield. Naturally, you would expect to win. But then, if you concede four, I guess you expect to lose. As the coach of Brazil once said, it doesn't matter if you let in four or five goals, as long as you score six or seven. I don't care if my team lets in four goals as long as we score five.

The balance of play swung like an uncontrollable see-saw, and so did our emotions: 0–1, 1–1, 2–1, 2–2, 3–2, 3–3, 3–4. It was pulsating. But that is why English football is so exciting. That is what endears me so much to the game here. I have to learn more about this side of English football. I know it's all useful in terms of looking ahead to the seasons to come. Games like this teach you the nuances of English football. Now I know I have to work hard!

Taking a wider view, on a normal day we would have

beaten Liverpool. But it was an abnormal game. It's difficult for the manager to speak to the team after a game like that. We played well, we scored goals, but we conceded four. How can you rebuke the defenders, but pat your midfield and forwards on the back and say well done? Kevin didn't do that because we are a team. It's a team game. Having said that, it was horrible on the coach coming back from Anfield. We had our fish and chips, but they left a sour taste this time. We were crestfallen. We had lost three games out of four. And all the while Manchester United kept winning. What made it even more staggering was that they seemed to win 1–0 in the last minute every game, whereas we fell into a nasty habit of succumbing to such untimely goals. A vexing, perplexing thought dawned on us, 'Hell, they've got a chance here.'

How come these last-minute goals never came our way? At Liverpool, with 10 minutes to go, we were winning 3–2. They scored twice in the last 10 minutes. At Blackburn, with five minutes to go, we were winning 1–0. They scored two in the last five minutes. We conceded too many goals in the crucial periods of a game. There are three key moments in a match: the first five minutes, the last five minutes of the first half and the last five minutes of the game. You can't be breached during these moments. It's kamikaze football and it saps morale. When I was younger I was taught that by a coach in France. I thought about it often this season.

If you have a goal against in the first five minutes, it's too quick. You have time to recover, but it takes a lot of will power and effort to come back into the game. If you have a goal against just before half time, you go back into the dressing room and feel mentally shaken, but you are having an enforced break. You might be dying to get out there and go at them but you have to tread water, and after half time, the rhythm of the game has often changed. And if you have a goal against in the last five minutes of the game, it's impossible to come back. Well, you only need to look at our faces at Anfield or Ewood Park to see the effect of that.

This is a very particular trait of English football. It is famous for its quickfire recoveries. You can be 3–1 up and lose 4–3 very quickly. English teams rarely admit defeat. As you say, it ain't over till it's over. There is always another chance. Until the referee's final whistle shrills, there is always the chance to score and you can win the game. It's different in France. If you are winning 3–1 with 15 minutes to go, it's all over. It will end 3–1. It's not that the players give up, or are resigned to it, it's just the way it is! But here, it's never finished. It might be 3–1 but you can win 5–3. Incredible. I'm learning about that resilience, it's a good addition to my game.

Another complication we faced was there were too many gaps in between games during the second half of the championship. I had my little break for a month and a half, then I came back and played one game, and then straight away there was another break for two weeks! Then another game followed by another 10-day pause. I couldn't get back into the groove. Keegan asked me, 'What's happening with you, David?' I always played 60 games a season, I was used to it from each of my years with PSG, but all the stopping and starting made it very difficult to keep my concentration, to keep the right amount of pressure and adrenaline.

During my last four seasons with PSG, we had a game every three days from November to May. If you're competing for the French Cup, league Cup, French championship, Europe, and the French national team, you're going to be busy. I always kept the pressure at a positive level. I didn't need to do too much training between games –

which suited me – but in Newcastle I feel I trained more than I played games. It's the first time my football had been that way. It can be very frustrating, especially if you lose a game. You desperately want to avenge that defeat but you might not have another game for two weeks. It's like having a car accident. If you don't get back into the car to drive as soon as possible, you are afraid. You never want to drive a car for your life.

When you have a setback, it's essential for your peace of mind to come back immediately. If you lose a game, and have to wait 10 or 15 days for the next game, you think too much. That's what happened to us. Manchester United had the FA Cup, which helped them to keep the pressure taut. They could forget about the championship while they concentrated on the Cup, and vice versa, and if you lose a league game on the Saturday and the next game is a victory in the FA Cup, you forget all about the game you lost in the league. But we had only the championship in our minds and as its value ballooned out of all proportion, so the tension soared. We had time on our hands playing only one competition. It was all too intense.

In France the league is the same size as in England, and in both countries there is a growing lobby for a smaller league, maybe comprising 18 teams. I think it will change in the future, which is a good thing, especially if you are in the Cups and Europe. But it's a double-edged sword. If, like Newcastle, you're tripped up in the Cup runs after a couple of strides, and there is no European competition, only 18 teams seems a pathetic number. Maybe we would have breaks of three weeks before the next game. Then we would all go crazy.

To prevent this, and to help me relax, I often listen to music in my free time. I love the fact that through evocative sounds you can take your mind into another world. I love music, especially the blues. Something groovy, very cool and relaxed, it makes me think about holidays, or hanging out with my friends in St Maxime. I love music which says, come with me, have fun, as if someone takes you by the shoulder and leads you into a happy place. I think people have to learn music. I want to learn to play an instrument because nothing can compare to what you can feel when you play an instrument, when you make a sound with your mouth or your fingers. I want to learn to play piano or guitar.

I listen to music every day, a different style depending on my mood. I love old jazz and classic blues, the likes of Buddy Guy, Melvin Taylor, Muddy Waters, BB King and John Lee Hooker. I dig the Rolling Stones and James Taylor. And I lose myself in the French sounds of Francis Cabrel, a blues guitarist and in my opinion the greatest singer in France. There is a Corsican band called I Muvrini who are very popular in the South of France. I admire their style because they sing their own music from their own region and culture, not an imported style from America. I like music that isn't taken from somewhere else. They sing about their land, their traditions, and of course they sing in their own language. They have made a name for themselves without being Americanised pop stars. When I hear their music I think of home.

Back at St James' Park, we tried to stoke up our assault on the title against QPR. It was another difficult game. When you are going for the championship, all the teams that come to your ground have something to prove. QPR were battling to stay in the Premier League, other teams were involved in the race for the title, others going for a place in Europe. You never play a team who has no motivation! There are no little teams. QPR wanted three points and they fought hard for them. Peter Beardsley scored two goals and we won the game, but until the final whistle blew I didn't think we were going to emerge victorious. The effects of late goals were still fresh and preying on our minds. We were feeling the mental strain of thinking about the race for the title permanently.

The curse of the last-minute goal reared its ugly head again 48 hours later. The Blackburn game was so bitterly disappointing, so deeply disheartening. We couldn't believe it had happened again. Leading 1–0 with five minutes to go, we didn't need binoculars to keep victory firmly in our sights. The contest was over. We worked bloody hard to take the lead and we were in control. And then . . . What's happening here? Again? It's like a jinx! We conceded a goal after 85 minutes, 1–1, and then another on 91 minutes. 1–2. Ninety one minutes? No way! We had three points. We had one point. Then we had no points at all. Unthinkable.

The self-belief and pluckiness we felt at the beginning of the season seemed like characteristics that belonged to another person. Our fortunes as the campaign reached its climax could not have struck a more direct contrast than the colours of the club. At the start of the season, sometimes we played badly and won games, now we were playing well and losing. The only important thing was to grab the points, and it seemed the harder we snatched at them, the later they were wrenched from us.

We recovered to string together three consecutive victories, all of them 1–0. What's this? Newcastle, the cavaliers, the famous swashbuckling attacking force, winning only 1–0? But who cares? The most important thing was to win the game. Even so, it was hard to find our old confidence again because the team we were battling against were ruthlessly consistent. Every time we left the pitch, having sweated for our points, our satisfaction was tainted when we learned Manchester United had won again. And again. And again.

We knew QPR would be spirited, but we didn't antici-
pate another edgy game against Aston Villa when they
visited St James'. They were fresh from winning the
League Cup, had a guaranteed European spot, were out of
the championship race and didn't really have anything to
prove. We expected an easy game. It wasn't. And we had to
win! The pressure was relentless, like someone holding a
knife against your throat.

CHAPTER FIFTEEN

Le Naufrage
Shipwreck

You're chasing the moon
Reaching out to touch the stars
But you land too soon.
What will it take to make you see
The way things really are?

The Lightning Seeds, 'Lucky You'

One week to go. We faced three games in six days. This mountain of a season reached its peak but it looked to be an implausible task that we would clamber to the very top. That would require a dramatic slip from our rivals from Old Trafford. The tension was palpable. The media were thoroughly enjoying a war of words between Kevin Keegan and Alex Ferguson. The Manchester United manager did his best to provoke a response from all the teams we faced in the title run-in. It was a battle of minds, nothing more. Keegan and Ferguson have a lot of respect for one another but when the pressure is at fever pitch and the prize is so close you can almost touch it, you do whatever is in your powers to help you grasp it. That's football. That's the game.

Sunday 28 April. We had a day off. My thoughts were with Nottingham Forest, who could do us a favour by beating Manchester United. I watched the game on television at home. After the first 25 minutes I fell asleep. I thought, 'This is very good, 0–0. A draw would be perfect.' When I woke up, with 15 minutes to go, it was 4–0 to Manchester United. I lay in my bed feeling very disappointed. We had to beat Leeds to stay in the race. We travelled to our hotel in Yorkshire.

Monday 29 April. Even though I was suspended, I went with the team to lend moral support. The atmosphere was the same as usual, a lot of jokes and banter. We trained in the morning, had a rest in the afternoon, and then went to the game. I watched the match sitting on the bench with Kevin Keegan and the lads. I shouted a lot. I understood how the manager feels when he is impotent on the sidelines even though he would dearly love to go onto the pitch to help. It's a strain on the heart.

I had reached 21 disciplinary points. You can't go against the law and that's the law. I have been booked more times in England than I ever was in France. The referees are more strict – especially with foreigners from France! Sometimes I really was amazed by the refereeing, I thought, 'Come on, surely you can't book me for this.' It reminded me of the mentality of the army. Ten press-ups when I say so! Stand there, do that . . .! We live in a democracy. Some referees are far too severe. But the most alarming thing was to discover some of the referees were rather happy to give me a yellow card. They showed me the yellow card with an ironic smile. The booking I can accept; the sardonic smile I can't accept. It's like saying, 'You French xxxx'.

The referee, first and foremost, loves football. They all

played football once. But some are like monsters. They are like policemen on the pitch to enforce the law. Come on, football is a game. I think you get more respect from the players if you are on the same level and not always being superior.

They are not all bad. Some referees have impressed me with their passion for the game, and if I show some great skill and they pass nearby, they say, 'Well done David, brilliant, that was world class.' I liked the referee from the game against Nottingham Forest, when we drew 1–1 in the penultimate game of the season. We had a laugh. I was so determined I went slightly over the top with one or two challenges, and rather than punishing me he said, 'David, be careful, I can't accept this.' I said, 'OK, fair point.' He dealt with the situation in a human way. I needed to calm down a bit and he had a quiet word with me. I respect that. It's better than the referees who go around with an attitude of 'I'm the boss and you can't say anything'. He just said, 'David you can't tackle like this.' He was right. We could smile about it. It isn't so much what you say as how you say it. The ref is a man like us, he is on the pitch like us. He tries to do his job like us. A referee can't be over-friendly with the players, but he isn't above the players either. The best referees are on the same level. We are all in the game together and we all have to play our part. OK, he has the yellow and the red cards in his pocket but as long as he treats me with respect, I will treat him with respect.

The referee who sent me off at Arsenal seemed very happy to send me off. He almost looked pleased to give me the first yellow card, that's for sure. He never warned me, he talked to Lee Dixon, and then turned round and gave me a yellow card. I am used to such behaviour now, it's normal.

I've experienced the same treatment from defenders. I

have come up against some defenders who say, 'You French bastard' during the game, in an attempt to destabilise me on the pitch. From the first minute, defenders can be provocative. They are doing their job, they have to stop the attacker. But then after the game, they shake hands and say, 'Well played David.' I have enjoyed playing against the different types of defenders in England. I found Rob Jones of Liverpool a very difficult opponent. I think he is a very good player and I like the fact that he plays hard but very fair. You have to respect everybody in your profession. I really need to feel that if I am going to be content in my football. That's the way I am. But if it reaches a point where I feel there are too many negative people, I will stop. I can't live in a world of hypocrisy. Most players love football, especially in England. There are so many players who may not be blessed with artistic quality, but they compensate with passion and generous effort. This is brilliant. It's not the same in France. The energy, the power of the game in England, is awesome.

That's the spirit of football here – play hard, be strong, then when the referee blows the whistle at the end, shake hands and go to have a drink at the bar. You are defending the colours of your club and you do everything in your power. But when it's finished, it's finished. You have to compare it to life. There are many similarities. There are laws and you have to know where to draw the line. Football is a great experience for life.

Tuesday 30 April. The team had a day off, but I trained as I hadn't played against Leeds. Then I went home to make my lunch, some duck with a green salad. I was alone in the house for the last month of the season because Coraline and the children went back to France. It was quiet and boring, but I knew it was good for my family to be in the South of France. I missed them and spent a lot of time on the phone.

Wednesday 1 May. We trained in the morning, then had lunch in the coach while we travelled to Nottingham for another game that we simply had to win. At this stage, a draw was not much better than a defeat. Three points was an urgent requirement. I always share a room with Keith Gillespie and to keep calm we watched snooker on TV.

Thursday 2 May. We went to Mansfield's Field Mill ground to train, returned to the hotel to have lunch, then we took a siesta before entering the last-chance saloon. Matchdays for footballers are ruled by a tight routine, designed so we feel comfortable and relaxed, with nothing to distract us from the game ahead. During the 90 minutes at the City Ground, our emotions were rocked like a sinking boat. From euphoria when Peter Beardsley scored to give us the lead, to shellshock as Forest equalised. We travelled back to Newcastle through the night, arriving at 2.30 in the morning. It was a coach of regrets. Quiet wasn't the word. Everybody connected with Newcastle was stunned. My mind flickered between numbness and pain, imagining and then blanking out elements of the game like a crackling silent movie. Kevin Keegan expressed his disappointment. I think Kevin realised in his head that it was finished, we had woken up from our dream.

It was difficult to be positive. But in retrospect I don't think it was right to lament this game. If we had to feel sorrow it should be about previous games that we lost. Sometimes a draw is fine if you can't win. A draw against Manchester United at home would have been sufficient. The same can be said of Blackburn and Liverpool away. That's football. For everyone who doesn't own a medal at the end of the season, it's one big if only.

I always keep regrets in my mind because if you remember your regrets you can live with more passion when you have a good experience. If we win next year, we will think about last season and enjoy it even more. Everybody wants this title.

Friday 3 May. Day off. I had to arrange everything for when I go back to France for the holidays. All the exciting things like paying all the bills. I made a few phone calls, took it very easy. You don't need to go out when there is one game to go. Mathematically it wasn't finished, but, but, but . . . it was a very difficult task. We had to rely on Manchester United losing, or if they drew, we had to get seven goals. A small chance. Of course, you have to have a will. For as long as the head can mathematically accept there is a chance you have to hope. But if I speak from my heart, it was before the Leeds match that I began to grasp the fact that it would take a miracle for us to overtake Manchester United.

Saturday 4 May. We trained in the morning and rested in the afternoon. I thought about our last game, due to take place in 24 hours' time. We knew that whatever we did, the title would be decided down the road at Middlesbrough. It was impossible to be positive. There was almost a sense of dread. In a way, I didn't want the game to happen because I wasn't looking forward to acknowledging the fact that the race was over and we had lost. Our fans didn't deserve that and I didn't want to see them depressed. It was difficult to see how we could celebrate coming second. The prospects of witnessing a Teesside miracle from Middlesbrough were as slim as a baguette.

Sunday 5 May. We met at the ground at 2.30 for a four o'clock kick-off. Before the game against Tottenham, Kevin Keegan was really upbeat in the team talk. The English have this remarkable resilience. If they lose a match, they brood over it briefly, and then instantly think positively about the next match. In France if you lose a match, days later people are still moaning about it. We had to win the game, but Tottenham made it hard for us because they were playing for a place in Europe. It was tough to go out onto the field and play. Very tough indeed. It's like two cars racing on a straight road, the black and white car takes a 100-yard lead, then with 50 yards to go he has an engine problem and the red car overtakes at the last moment. It is soul-destroying for the black and white car to complete the last 50 yards after that. He'll do it but it's very sad because if you are convinced you will win the race, you can't accept losing. We drew 1–1, but it was irrelevant as Manchester United won 3–0. I had finished runner-up before, but always had the consolation of a cup. This was more galling.

At the end of the game, we went on a lap of honour. I wanted to say thank you to the Geordies for everything they had given to me in my first season. I had expected it to be more difficult than it really was to play in Newcastle. But the reality was it was so easy because the fans were tremendous. I suddenly realised I was on my own on the pitch. I thought all the lads were behind me but they had gone back to the dressing room and I was alone! But I wanted to thank everyone. And I'll say it again now to all the Toon Army: 'Cheers mate'.

The team draws so much of its strength from the fans. Definitely. Monaco are a great example of how opposite things can be in France. It's a big club, they are a strong team that attracts world-class players, like Glenn Hoddle and Jürgen Klinsmann who both played for Monaco recently. Yet for every game there are only 5,000 fans in the stadium. If at every game you play at home there is no atmosphere in the stadium, you can't give of your best. The mood of boredom is infectious, it's harder to get the adrenaline pumping. In Newcastle it's the opposite and it's tremendous.

The Newcastle fans are brilliant. They are very passionate, and they were only friendly to me from the moment I signed. It wasn't the same in Paris. When you are playing football, being in a passionate environment is such an advantage – it's what you look for – and I found this in Newcastle. The fans are always at the club, always around the players. The fans come to the training ground in far greater numbers than I was used to in France. They want success and that rubs off on you. If you are having a bad game they push you to find your best form; if you lose, the next game they are here in force, full of encouragement. It's inspirational.

I was even more aware of their commitment to the cause when we played away from St James' Park. In London, at QPR for example, we feel like we're playing at home. There are more black and white shirts than the blue and white hoops. In a working-class town people identify with football. United are the focal point of the community. It's the same in Lens and Lille in France, which are also working-class mining towns and the people are much warmer and more passionate. Football is the big Saturday outing, it's the important moment of the week. Whereas in Paris and in London, there are other pastimes, other options for people's amusement. Football is a different world to all other sports. For football fans, it's more of a religion than a pastime. It has a bigger place in the heart of the people. It is the game of the people.

Some of the Newcastle fans carry a tricolour flag, the red, white and blue of France, and that makes me feel very proud. They are very receptive about what I do on the pitch. I was very surprised to be accepted so quickly. They make me even more keen to give my best, to respond to their emotions. You always have pressure, especially when you want to win something and I take the support and expectation of the Toon Army as positive pressure. It pushes me further. That is why I felt so sorry that we didn't deliver the title they were entitled to. They were so desperate for it and they had waited so many years for success. I hope they have it very soon.

That fact that we missed something great, something very, very great, weighed heavy in my soul. On the Sunday night, everything I had in the back of my mind came rushing to the front, all the experiences. You can win or you can lose, but you can't forget all the twists and turns of the season.

Some people have equilibrium – if things are good or bad they stay on an even keel. Not me. If we win the title next year it will be even better because we know what it means to miss it. It was so heartbreaking for the Geordie lads in the team – Peter Beardsley was disconsolate – but for Lee Clark and Steve Watson, they are very young. They think we will do it next season and they have plenty of time to drink the sweet taste of success. Peter is an example to everybody at Newcastle, especially the young players. He is 35 years old and plays like a 20-year-old. He is a great professional who works very hard every day. I think he has a good mentality for the club. He's a good captain, one of the players who pushes the team all the time. Look at him, he's 35 and he doesn't sit back, he still practises diligently. If you are young and you watch Peter Beardsley you think, 'I have to move my arse because look at him. At 35 he's still going strong. He knows what he wants.' I hope I can go on to 35. When I watch Peter I think maybe he can play football until he's 40.

Kevin Keegan told us we had played a great season, he realised we had made too many mistakes to finish first, but urged us not to be too disappointed with second place. He encouraged us to be happy about what we achieved, to feel proud of ourselves and our progress. But I realised in his voice he was desperately sad. If you try to give a positive message when your voice is cracking, it doesn't necessarily have the intended impact. I was more upset for him than I was for me. He looked so upset. I came off the pitch and when I saw him I was so sad for him. I was sad for me, too, but the look on his face really brought home the reality of what we had missed out on. I really wanted to give him the title.

Kevin Keegan wears his heart on his sleeve. Apart from being a great trainer he is a great guy. If you're not a big character, you can't be a great manager. He has so many qualities – he is interested in people, he listens to you, he is always available to talk to, he doesn't hide his emotions, he's honest and he's loyal. He's been a great example to me, and I would recommend to any player he is a fine person to be around, to learn from, in terms of football and as a man. He was a massive star but he is a good person on a human level, too. If I were to be a manager, Keegan is someone I would try to imitate. I would also model myself on Artur Jorge. They are both people who have an innate understanding of the job. They know how to do things the right way. All these qualities – genuine human qualities – either you have them or you don't. It's not something you can acquire.

What is the recipe for a great manager? When you are a great footballer, anyone can master technique, but man-management skills is where a good trainer comes into his own. You can't inspire a group of individuals in the same way. One might be sensitive, one thick-skinned, yet they are within the group and the key to effective management is to get the individuals to perform within the team environment. They must play to the best of their own abilities but for the greater benefit of the team. Today, any manager of a successful club is a manager of group dynamics, his job is to put all the diverse talents together, aiming in the same direction. You can teach people to strive for technical perfection but if you don't understand the personalities, you may as well forget it.

I was angry to see the press attacking Keegan when we started to lose points. As our 12-point lead began to diminish bit by bit, Keegan became a bigger scapegoat in the eyes of the media. They got it completely wrong as far as Kevin is concerned. Keegan and McDermott, in their minds, wanted to do the best they possibly could for the club. It happens that people make errors of judgement. We are not robots. But a journalist's job is not to understand that, their job is to create an explosion. We should try to see it in a more intelligent way. The press didn't look, and then think. Instead of analysing, suggesting Keegan made a decision because he thought it would strengthen us here or be good for the team there, they just went for the jugular. They didn't try to understand why these things happened. They preferred to convey: this is what happened, it's a grave mistake, and he's no good. What a blinkered outlook.

It was crazy to see some of the so-called 'experts' blaming Faustino Asprilla for the fact we lost the title. If you look at the results since Tino arrived – played 14, won 6, drawn 3, lost 5, compared to before he came – played 24, won 18, drawn 3, lost 3, you can see our form slumped. The facts show we lost approximately one in three games compared to one in eight games before he arrived. But come on! That wasn't the fault of Tino, that was the fault of the team. I know more than most that you don't point the finger at one man for a team's disappointments. Football is about human beings, not statistics. Football is about movement and the flow of the game, the fine balance on which supremacy and submission on a football field teeters, not mathematics. If we, as a team, had concentrated more in certain games where we threw away a lead, no one would have criticised Tino. We would have won the league, and he, like all the other players in the team, would have been celebrated.

At the beginning of the season, Kevin Keegan was football's hero, extolling all the virtues of the beautiful game. At the end of the season, according to the media, he had lost Newcastle the league. I can't be like that. I can't say everything is perfect and then about turn and claim it's disastrous. Football isn't black and white like that. It isn't right to go to such extremes. You can't say that at the beginning of the season he was the genius and at the end of the season he was foolish. But Keegan himself warned me to be guarded about the media.

I have found it irritating that everyone in England seems so obsessed by the relationship between Eric Cantona and me. The reason the media create this whole hype about a rift between us is just to sell newspapers, no question. It's economical in terms of selling newspapers and, more importantly, it's economical in terms of the truth. They sell more papers, that's the only justification. The whole story is annoying. It's as if they simply have to find something to say just because we are both French and both playing in the same league in England. That's the whole basis for everything that is written or said about us. It doesn't mean we hate each other. But, at the same time, just because we are both French that doesn't mean we have to be bosom buddies either.

So, Cantona's team won the league and mine didn't. Steve Bruce's team won the league and Steve Howey's team didn't! It's the same thing, isn't it? In my mind, I don't care who wins the league if it wasn't us. Whether it was Man United or Bolton made no difference. The hurt wasn't enhanced because it was Eric. It only hurt because it wasn't Newcastle.

But you have to go forward. We will be stronger and more experienced for next year. You have to learn from everything that happens in your life. I never live with the past haunting me in my head. I always use the past as experience and turn a negative into a positive. Make sure I don't make the same mistake again. If we have learned one thing about last season it's that it's never over till it's over. That goes both for the entire championship race and the 90 minutes of a single game. I have gained a lot from my first experiences in the Premier League. I know now the attitude of the managers and the players, the referees and the fans. I am more capable of adapting mentally to the rigours of the English season now.

Suddenly we were on holiday. We missed the Championship, the FA Cup, the Coca-Cola Cup. We missed everything. It was a weird sensation. All those plans for a Geordie knees-up were scuppered. Newcastle would have been electric had we had the Premiership trophy to parade. But how could we have a party? The prospect of seeing the fans and talking to everyone about missing out on something special was a hellish thought. Too damned painful.

We couldn't just stop our lives because we weren't champions. I had some friends over from France and we went back to my house. There was a present waiting for me on my doorstep when I got back. It was some beers. There was a message attached: 'To David, You are the best. You have given your best all the way through the season. I give you some French beer and one pack of French cigarettes for your party tonight.' It made me smile. I made some telephone calls to my family in France and then we had a drink in the garden because it was a beautiful balmy night. Of course I felt depressed, but after three or four beers the pain lessened. I wanted to put my misery to one side because I wanted my friends to have a good time in Newcastle. I wanted to say to them 'I'm with you.' I didn't want them feeling they had to treat me with kid gloves.

Some young lads still bedecked in the black and white

shirt came to my house to speak to me. They were very cool. We shared a sense of all having lost something together. There was no aggression or blame. In France, if you lose, the fans want to argue with you, 'How did you lose? How could you?' But in England, the fans were more upset than the players. We had to console them more than the fans consoling us! This amazed me. Then one of my friends asked me for a football and we had a night-time kick-about in the garden. That was the end of my season.

CHAPTER SIXTEEN

Le Calme après l'Orage
The Calm after the Storm

Way down South there's a clear stream running
In the night I feel my heart turning
I'm feeling some day I'd like to come
Back to the place I started from,
Take it home.

BB King, 'Take It Home'

The lads went to Cyprus to have an end-of-season holiday. I didn't want to turn them down, and I think it would have been great to wind down from the season we had, all of us together. But the timing was wrong for me. I explained to them, 'I really want to go with you but I also need to go back and see my family.' They understood. After six weeks away from my wife and children, I was eager to get to France. As a foreigner, there are times in the year when you need to be at home, with your old friends, speaking your own language. No pressure, no insecurity. Everything is totally familiar and comfortable.

I went back to the South of France with one thought in

my head: not a post mortem on the championship, not a daydream about France's squad for Euro 96, not a sadness that I wouldn't see any Brown Ale for two months. My only concern was having a good time.

I got onto the plane, St Maxime-bound after a mind-blowing year. I said to myself, 'David, I wish you a nice holiday!' Nothing complicated. All I wanted was to cherish time with my family, see all my friends, and revive the soul. I woke up early in the morning so I could enjoy the whole day. I wanted to see the sun rise in the blue sky. This ball of yellow peeps out from the sea and glides over the horizon and it's so beautiful. I didn't want to sleep in and lose half the day. Stay in bed until noon, and if I want to play golf, which takes four hours, then there is no time for the beach. Tough life, huh? I might play golf in the morning, have lunch with all the family, go to the beach in the afternoon. I can get so much from the day. I like to fill my day with excitement, then have a good sleep to feel refreshed. When you know that the sun goes down deep into the evening, at 10 at night, you have a very good day. This is how I like to spend my holiday. Relaxed but enriching. Go fishing sometimes, go into the country visiting all the villages, go back to my college in Nice, go walking in the mountains in Italy with my son and my father.

This life helped me to come back to England stronger. I wanted to come back feeling like a winner. I needed to accumulate a lot of things in my mind and my body to come back refreshed. I demanded more energy and spark from myself, with the batteries inside me fully recharged. At the end of the season, the batteries had been drained until they were empty.

Although I have a very different lifestyle in Newcastle and St Maxime, I am always the same. Maybe a bit more tranquil in St Maxime. I have no pressure there. In the season, I work, and I have to be focused. When I'm on holiday I want to be cool all the time. Take my time to really enjoy things. I have a scooter to get around when I'm in St Maxime, yet even on that I don't whiz around like a maniac. It's good to slow down for a while. I never considered taking a holiday in England, when you go on holiday you need a change of scene. Look where the English go to on holiday – they go to Tenerife, to the sun and the heat. I couldn't be on holiday in England, because that's where I work and I need my change of scene, too. I love going back to St Maxime. It's my home town. I know every nook and cranny. I can jump on my motorbike and drive everywhere in the whole place. It's better for zipping around, especially in the high season when the road from St Tropez to St Maxime is like the M25.

During the summer I was invited to all sorts of events. I had propositions to go to see the NBA in America, the Grand Prix, the Tennis Open. If I wanted, I could go every week to another sporting extravaganza. I chose the ones I really wanted to do. I couldn't possibly attend them all, otherwise I would have spent the entire summer in aeroplanes and airports and I could do without looking for matchsticks to keep my eyes open. So I'm picky. I get to have a good time and still enjoy enough rest so I am ready for the season ahead.

I went to the Grand Prix in Monaco and Barcelona. Formula One never ceases to thrill me. I was always a great admirer of Ayrton Senna. I am taken aback by the technology and the sheer speed. The difference between seeing it live and watching it on TV is massive. In Monaco, I was invited to see the Williams team and I met Frank Williams. He said, 'My wife is a Geordie. I'm going to Newcastle tomorrow – why don't you come with me?' All the men in the pit are football fans, some Manchester United, Liverpool and Newcastle, a happy mix! Everyone wanted to talk about football and we had a good laugh. I haven't been in a Formula One car myself, but I have driven round a circuit. It's one of the bonuses of being a famous footballer, you get to try all the things you dreamed about. I'm very lucky.

Although I had no medal to take home I did have three awards. I finished third in the two annual football awards voted for by the players and the football writers. That was a boost in my first season. Maybe if I had played better after Christmas I could have been higher.

I won one other award during the season, for 'Head of the Year'. It is a hairdressing award for the most stylishly groomed coiffure. One day I went into training and I told Kevin the news. He said, 'It's a good thing. I have received this award before. Go and have a good time.' Everyone knows about Kevin Keegan and his famous hairstyles.

I gave all the shirts I have collected in my career away. I always keep one as a souvenir of all my clubs and all the clubs I have played against, but all the medals are for me. My private things.

I had a few weeks to wait for the announcement of the France squad for the European Championships. I was pretty much resigned to the fact I wouldn't be hurrying back to England. My last appearance for the national team had been as a substitute in a 10–0 win over Azerbaijan in a Euro 96 qualifying game in September 1995. The only thing that gave me a glimmer of hope was the reaction of other people. Everyone around me was telling me it was possible but deep down, I knew it was a lost cause. My friends, and even strangers I met in the street, were saying, 'Oh come on David, he has to take you . . .' In my head, I didn't really believe it, but if that's all you hear you naturally begin to think, 'Well maybe they aren't all completely wrong.' But they were. When Aimé Jacquet selected his squad I thought, 'OK, I am on holiday now.'

I wasn't going to feel terrible about it. I wasn't going to beg the guy! If he didn't choose me, he didn't choose me. Look at me. I'm sitting at the *plage des éléphants*, the elephant beach. It's named in honour of the mythical stories of Babar, whose author, Jean de Brunhoff, lived in the house which overlooks this stretch of sand. I'm enjoying the sunshine and the sea, some fresh fish and a glass of rosé, do I look like I'm having a terrible time here? Do you think I felt sad about it? Life was not too bad! I'm not going to put a bullet through my head just because I didn't get picked for the French team. That's the way it is. Who was it who sang, 'Always look on the bright side of life?' (Feel free to whistle the rest.)

Look at that guy over there. He's got his feet in the water. You can imagine you are in there with him in the little rocky bay. He's fishing for shellfish. The sun's glow bounces around on the sea. The shafts of sun cut through the branches on the trees and highlight the houses in the hills. It's quiet, *tranquille*. Look at how beautiful it is. To my eyes, it's a perfect image. My good friend Fabien pours a drink at his bar on the beach. He has travelled all over the world, and when he returns he enchants us with stories of all the wonderful places he has seen. But he always reaches the same conclusion: we live in the most beautiful place. This is St Maxime. This is where I spent my summer. It wasn't so bad.

I can't say I don't care that I didn't play in Euro 96. Of course I'm disappointed. I didn't watch the matches because, frankly, if I did I knew I would be inclined to get into a bad mood. After all, it is my job and my country, and that is where my heart will always lie. But I wasn't prepared to drive myself completely crazy worrying about it. What is the point in sulking?

For the entire duration of the summer, none of my family spoke to me about football. They know I'm sad.

They know I'm disappointed to have lost the league, they know I wanted to be in the French team. They know everything. But they also know that I need something else. I need something different to throw myself into. We speak about everything except football. Even if there is a game on we do our best to ignore it.

I didn't go to England for Euro 96. I didn't even watch much of it on the television in France. But I watched England. They played well and made a sensational spectacle. Everyone in France was very impressed and told me what a pleasure it was to watch the English team on the pitch. Whereas other teams were afraid to attack, England were committed to it. The French were quite surprised. I looked at them in amazement: of course the English team is great to watch. I had told them often enough, it's an excellent league which breeds exciting footballers! What did they expect?

I didn't watch France play, except for the penalties against the Czech Republic in the semi-finals. France didn't play football in this game. The only thing to depress me was the thought of France playing at St James' Park. I couldn't watch it. I was on holiday. I didn't want to put a knife through my heart. I didn't need to rub salt into the wounds. That was my stadium and my country. I didn't want to think about it at all. Despite all the hurt I felt after the France v Bulgaria situation, it never dashed my patriotism. Because France is always in my heart – even now.

I didn't know people in England were quizzing the manager Aimé Jacquet about me and Cantona. It was never mentioned in the press in France. I didn't really care. I was at home with my family and I wasn't prepared to ruin our fun. I wouldn't say I forgot about football, but I was relieved to keep my distance.

I was sorry to see England go out on penalties. It's terrible for the players who have to take them but at the same time, it's the rules. You can't condemn a penalty shoot-out as unjust for the losers and claim it as justified for the winners. It's always the same – ecstasy for the team who win and agony for the team who lose. It just depends which side you're on! I have taken many penalties before. I was the designated penalty taker for my previous clubs. It's impossible to express what you feel, facing the goalkeeper from 12 yards with everyone in the ground focused on you. You feel alone, you feel all the responsibility on your shoulders. It can be a mind-blowing experience. I think I have missed only one. I have experienced losing in a penalty shoot-out – Newcastle felt it last season in the FA Cup – but I imagine that's nothing compared to a European Championship or a World Cup. It's not the same pressure as knowing millions of people are transfixed all around the world as you kick for football's ultimate prize.

Euro 96 saw the introduction of the golden goal. As a footballer you have to respect all the new rules. I'm sure all the Germany players feel it's a positive step for football, but all the players from the Czech Republic must think it's dreadful. During the decade that I have played football professionally, there has been a new suggestion for a rule modification every year. Each year a new situation: the offside rule, the tackle from behind, the golden goal, enlarging the goals, alternatives for the penalty shoot-out, the throw in, you name it, someone somewhere isn't satisfied. In all that time, only two rules have changed.

But there is one major adjustment which I believe is imminent, which will have a radical effect on the game. I expect it's only a matter of time before we see a fourth official in the stands with a TV monitor, like they have in American football. As they say, we have the technology, so why not? We can eliminate big mistakes. At the end of the day the referee is a man not a robot. There is so much money at stake in football now and that leads to enormous knock-on pressure. Some teams literally can't afford to lose a game and if they are denied by a false decision, it's terrible for the referee. As the financial input grows, it gets harder and harder to officiate a game. Referees need help. It's not fair to say all refs are bad, just that they need assistance. I hope it happens.

But it would be a massive step for football to take. We have to be mindful of stopping the game the whole time. In America, every time the referee blows his whistle to stop the game there is an advert on the TV. We can't have that in football. If we have a second referee we will have to change the whole mentality of football.

It's important not to change everything. We mustn't lose track of the beautiful simplicity of the game. You can tinker with the rules, but you can't change the essence of the game. Football is still football. It's in good shape. It's a great sport. It's the sport of the world. I will always think that and as long as there are a lot of spectators who come to see the game, there is your proof.

In my St Maxime haven, I thought about the title race from time to time. I had to, because people in France kept asking me about it. We were so close. We were so agonisingly close to the title. To their eternal credit, although the Newcastle fans were devastated by it, many of them rallied round to say, 'It's OK. Second is not bad. We're still in Europe.' The enormity of the disappointment only sunk in during the close season.

Looking back at the conclusion of the championship, of course I feel dejected. I remember thinking, when we were knocked out of both the Cups, 'Well at least we're 10 points clear of Manchester United, and if we win the championship it will be brilliant.' It was cockiness born out of ambition rather than arrogance, but it sounds inane now. Of course we feel low about throwing away the championship. But I don't want any sense of regret to linger for too long. It's not very good for you or the people who love you and are around you.

It's hard to compare the feeling to anything. I lost the championship the same way in France too. PSG were second to Marseille, only two points behind. Chris Waddle's team won, our great rivals. If you finish sixth and you weren't even close to the championship it doesn't hurt so much. You try to get a place in Europe and look ahead to next year. But finishing second, after being 12 points clear of Man United with a couple of months to go? You don't feel the burden of many bigger regrets than that.

I don't want to be despondent. That's life, I say. All the Newcastle fans know we tried everything. You can criticise our tactics if you like, but you can't criticise our effort. But some of the people in France were mystified. They said to me, 'David, you had a 10-point lead, what happened?' They can't understand it, but they have to. Everyone who is interested in football asks me: 'You had so many points ahead of Manchester and you lost the title . . . Why?' It gets very boring having to explain it all the time. I would prefer it if I had the championship medal in my pocket and everyone was patting me on the back and saying, 'Brilliant.'

So what was the problem? The key factor was inconsistency. We didn't play very well after Christmas on a regular basis. We played well for one game or for one half but we weren't consistent. That was the difference between us and Manchester United. I can't explain why we couldn't maintain the standards we set at the beginning of the season. There is no reason. We didn't change our style, our methods, our attitude. We made mistakes we hadn't made before on the field. Why, I don't know. People who know how to drive and always control the car the same way sometimes have a crash. Why, I don't know. People who eat every day and know how to use cutlery sometimes spill their food. Why, I don't know. Maybe it is just a question of concentration. When you are leading a game of football with minutes to go, it's essential to keep your concentration if you want to protect that lead.

I have experienced close championships before in France, but it was more difficult in England because I am a foreigner. There is clearly more emphasis on foreign players to perform, more expectation, and if there are problems, the finger of blame is pointed more easily at me than another player. That's something to accept about playing in another country.

For me, this season was black and white in so many ways. It was exhilarating before Christmas, then exacting after. It was especially difficult when I was banned. I lost my rhythm, I lost everything I worked for since arriving in England. I think I played some good games before the ban, and to stay one and a half months away from the pitch obscured my focus, all the spirit and confidence that I had before was diminished. Mentally, the ban caused a lot of damage, too much. It felt like I cut something. The sense of timing was as warped as a Salvador Dali. I had been playing well and scored a couple of goals, and after the ban, that was it. I didn't recover my football, or my confidence. I don't know why, but I wasn't taking players on as often. I needed the summer holidays to clear my head so I could start afresh the following season.

My greatest strength is that I will never be beaten by someone. I will never be beaten by a situation. Whenever I face a difficult moment I find something in my mind and in my body to push all those problems away. In football you have to be mentally strong and that's not always easy.

I suppose my worst fault is that I always think I am right. Sometimes I have to admit I played shit. Sometimes the manager comes to me and says, 'You were rubbish today.' What? Me? Rubbish? Surely not. I have to learn to see it, to recognise the faults in my game so I can do something about them. Kevin Keegan advises me how I should add to my game. He tells me some things which are very effective in France need to be altered to work here. He encourages me to keep the best qualities in my game and work on all the rest! You change every minute you play on the pitch, every game, every season. You have to change if you want to progress. You can never stand still or people will catch you up.

I have to admit I am not really a wide man. I didn't know being an orthodox winger was part of the plan when I signed, but I don't have a problem with that. When I arrived we tried all sorts of positions, all the players did, and Kevin Keegan said, 'This season it's best for the team if we play with two out-and-out wingers and two up front.' I thought it was a good idea. I didn't want to tell him I prefer playing a freer role. He is the manager and he makes the decisions. But he did say towards the end of the season, maybe next year I would play more central. I hope so.

I was the second attacker playing just off George Weah with Paris Saint-Germain, with more freedom to attack through the heart of the opposition's resistance. I prefer playing that role, because I have more possibilities to score goals. I played in midfield against Arsenal this season and I scored, and against Nottingham Forest I scored and made an assist from a more central area. But I have played on the wing to fit into the tactical system at Newcastle. When we were at our most potent as a team, we played with two wingers and two centre forwards: Peter Beardsley and Les Ferdinand up front, me and Keith Gillespie on the wings. That was Keegan's plan. But truthfully, it would be easier to play in my old position. When you play on the wing you have to stay by the touchline all the time. I enjoy playing with more space.

Maybe we'll buy more players but, looking at the season, a bigger squad isn't necessarily the answer. We played well, we just have to concentrate on our quality and our team spirit. We have a lot to look forward to – a renewed attack on the league, the cups and Europe. We have to play well in the different competitions. Season 1996-97 will be extremely important to us.

Just as I was preparing to return to England for pre-season training, the Barcelona bombshell broke. A year after their abortive attempt to sign me from PSG, they approached Newcastle for my signature. Joining Barcelona had always been a dream and I couldn't believe they came for me again. In the end, the Spanish bid failed because the two clubs couldn't agree a fee. Newcastle wanted a lot of money and Barcelona offered less than the asking price.

You feel very proud and excited if you have a great club who wants to buy you, and when it all came to nothing I was a little disappointed. Everything, it seemed, would have been perfect for me: to play with a great club, to be 40 minutes by plane or a four-hour drive from my home in St Maxime, to be in a climate which is bathed in sunshine, to enjoy the lifestyle of a southern European city . . . it was an especially promising proposition for my family.

Newcastle is a great club but they are not yet on the same scale as Barcelona – maybe they will be there in a few years time, but not now. I am nearly 30 years old and I don't know how many chances I will have to play on such a stage. I can't be sure I will still be playing when Newcastle attain the status their ambition craves. I have faith they will get there, but it takes time to become one of the best clubs in the world and to establish such a reputation.

It wasn't that I wanted to leave Newcastle because I

wasn't happy at the club! It's not that I don't love the club or the fans, it's simply because the proposal from Barcelona was fantastic for me personally. It's not like I would go to Middlesbrough or Southampton or something. Barcelona, alongside AC Milan, Ajax Amsterdam and Real Madrid, is one of the select few clubs at the pinnacle of the international game. It's among *la crème de la crème*. Their history is undisputed – Barcelona have won the Spanish championship 14 times and the cup 22 times! They have won all three European trophies. The Nou Camp stadium holds more than 100,000. With the greatest respect to Newcastle, I really want the Geordies to understand why I was tempted. By wanting to go to Barcelona I was looking after my interests and ultimately Newcastle were looking after theirs too. That's business.

As for all the stories in the newspapers saying that I wanted to leave because my house in Newcastle was burgled – what utter rubbish. Of course, I wasn't ecstatic to have suffered from a robbery, but to suggest that was 'the final straw' is complete nonsense. My house in Paris was burgled when I was on my holidays from PSG. That's life, it happens.

Newcastle were approached by a few other clubs, but neither the board nor myself wanted to encourage their interest in me. If I have a message for the Geordies it's that I didn't want to leave for another English club because I think Newcastle is the best club in England now. But to be approached by Barcelona was something awesome for me. I am at the peak of my career and it was a fabulous opportunity. The World Cup in 1998, in France, is another consideration. If I went to Barcelona it would enhance my chances of getting back into the French squad. Playing in Newcastle makes it more difficult for me to play for the national team. I don't know why, but that seems to be the case.

Barcelona have a huge reputation in France. But it's more than that – it's all around the world – they are recognised as one of *the* special football clubs. When I went to Newcastle the French said, 'Where is Newcastle?' but everyone knows the tradition of Barcelona. Knowing I had the chance to play for one of the best clubs in the world, I will never be the same now in my mind. Something very important to me is gone now. I have to get used to that.

I was uncertain as to how everyone in Newcastle would react to the situation. I was delighted to find, as usual, the attitude of the fans was brilliant. They were all very happy to see me again! Naturally there was a barrage of questions – Are you staying? Are you going? Is it true? Is it just paper talk? Everyone wanted a personal answer. My response was that I just wanted to play football. The Barcelona deal was dead, all over. I came back to work committed to giving 100 per cent to my job and to my club. I am a professional and that was the only thing I wanted to focus on. It was reassuring to get out onto the field and play. When I am on the pitch I don't think about anything else except playing football to the very best level I can.

The players and the staff didn't go on about it. It's very difficult to speak to someone about transfer speculation. Everyone returned to training in a very positive frame of mind, looking ahead to next season. I am just concentrating on having a great year in Newcastle.

Transfer activity of a different kind dominated everyone's thoughts a week after I got back to the North East with the dramatic arrival of Alan Shearer, a world-class goalscorer and a Geordie to boot. It was a fantastic boost for everyone connected to the club and I am sure it will make us a stronger force for the campaign ahead. Our squad is looking good and we will go for glory both in England and abroad.

172

I hope Newcastle will raise a few European eyebrows next year. When I played in Paris, we surprised a lot of people in European competition. The first season we played in Europe we beat Napoli 2–0 in Italy. That was great. People were saying, 'Can you believe about Paris? Did you see them? They were bloody brilliant!' With the quality of the players and the mentality of the team, I think Newcastle have a great chance of making an impact in Europe. But the pressure is on. You don't have many chances in European football. You have only two games, home and away, to perform if you want to go through to the next round. It's just a question of preparing your mind. You know you won't get a lot of chances, then if you get one, you have to take it. You can't be scared of a chance.

I was in Europe every year with Paris Saint-Germain. We played some of the great teams in Europe: Barcelona, AC Milan, Napoli, Real Madrid, Juventus, Arsenal, Bayern Munich, Dinamo Kiev, Spartak Moscow. I love playing in Europe and I missed it in my first year in Newcastle. Especially when we were knocked out of the FA and Coca-Cola Cups very early and then sometimes had to go two or three weeks without a game. That gets very boring. When you have Europe as well as your domestic games, it's non-stop action, and if offers a refreshing change of scene and impetus. You don't have any time to get nervous or stale. You just focus on the game on Saturday, then focus on the game on Wednesday, then Saturday. You don't have any time to get tired because you are concentrating on your game so intensely. You don't train very hard between the games, just prepare yourself mentally. I thrive on that.

The spirit of PSG drove us to success and bound all the different personalities together. There is a clear parallel. If anything, the spirit at Newcastle is stronger. The players are closer. The English players have obviously got more in common with one another, so from time to time the foreigners might feel a little bit on the outside. It's not a case of the English players sticking together and the foreigners sticking together, but it's natural that people have more affinity with their own compatriots. Sometimes I think it would be nice to go out one night with some French people just to have a laugh. Humour is the most difficult thing to translate – I don't always understand English jokes and the English don't often comprehend mine. Which is probably just as well!

But the amazing thing about football is the game's ability to cross all barriers. You can be overwhelmed with an incredibly intense football experience and it doesn't matter if you are in England, in France, in Japan, in Mongolia, it's breathtaking. It's a universal togetherness.

My ambitions for next season are to win the league, have a good adventure in Europe and to make people happy. To have a good life, good health and to enjoy the life in Newcastle even more. Not very complicated things. Sometimes I dream about playing for France in the World Cup in 1998. I have a beautiful vision that we will win, I hope I see it for real. But my true ambition is to have happiness in my life.

Where do I see myself in 10 years' time? Not far from St Maxime I guess, but I don't know and I don't care. Now I am a footballer, I have my family, I have my house. In 10 years' time, wait and see. If I couldn't play any more I would go to the scrapyard, get hold of some metal to tie around my ankles and I'd jump in to the sea to wait for the sharks! 'I'm here! Come on, come and get me!' But seriously, people expect you to fall apart when you stop playing. Obviously, I am not looking forward to that time but I won't worry about it or plan ahead. When the time comes – and touch wood it's in the distant future – I'll simply do something else.

Index

Note: The abbreviation DG is used in the index to denote David Ginola.

AC Milan 17–18, 48, 70, 91
Albert, Philippe 133
alcohol 112–13
Arsenal 29, 48, 92, 98, 105
  interest in DG 69, 89,
    93
  v. Newcastle 135, 136
  Coca-Cola Cup match
    123, 124–6, 128, 147
Asprilla, Faustino 3, 71,
    98, 131, 155
Association Sportive
    Maximoise 5–6, 28
Azerbaijan 162

Barcelona club
  1995 48–9, 86
  interest in DG 90,
    170–72
Bardot, Brigitte 7
Barton, Warren 101, 110
Bastia 66

Batty, David 97, 98
Baudelaire, Charles
  L'Albatross 22, 69
Bayern Munich 49
Beardsley, Peter 98, 141,
    149, 153, 169
Beckenbauer, 37
Bergkamp, Dennis 92
Bernès, Jean-Pierre 44
Bjekovic, Nenad 27–8
Bolton 118
Bonnemain, Mme.
    (schoolteacher) 15
Bordeaux 27
Bourrier, Marc 28
Brazil 86, 137
Brest club 35–9, 84, 96
Bulgaria 28
  v. France 1993 63–5

Cabannes, Laurent 58
camphor oil 1, 5–6

Cantona, Eric 35, 52, 63, 64, 82, 92, 104
  and Marseille 43–4
  at Selhurst Park 127
  relations with DG 156, 164
Celtic 89, 91, 104
Cerruti, Nino 57–8
Chaker, Charly 38
Chelsea 123
Clark, Lee 153
Clarkson, Ian 124
Coca-Cola Cup 124–6, 128, 147
Collymore, Stan 3
Colombia 71
commercial opportunities 54–9
Courbis, Rolland 69
Coventry City 117
Cox, Neil 119
Cruyff, Johan 37, 49, 90
Cup-Winners' Cup 69, 87, 92
Czechoslovakia 164, 165

Dalger, Christian 25, 26–7
Dallinger, Adam, poem by 117
De Chavane, Christophe 56
Dein, David 93
Denisot, Michel 69–70, 89
Dinamo Kiev 49
Disney World 77
diving 123–4

Dixon, Lee 124–5, 126, 147
Djorkaeff, Youri 68

Edinburgh 104
England team 28–9, 164–5
Escobar, Andres 71
European Championships 48, 173
  1984 16–17
  1990 36
  1996 162–5
European Cup 45, 83, 87
  1977 17, 95
  1990 35
  1992 44
  1995 48–9, 86
  1996 68

FA Cup 123, 140, 165
fans 2, 110, 151–3, 157–8, 166, 167, 172
  women 113
Ferdinand, Les 2, 92, 97, 101, 119–20, 123, 169
Ferguson, Alex 145
Fernandez, Luis 31, 33, 80–4, 86, 89
films 22, 61–2
Fletcher, Freddie 91
France
  food 112
  nuclear tests 111
  see also Paris; St Maxime; St Tropez

French Cup 35, 42, 45
  1993 46
French Football Federation
  37, 44–5
  club system 96, 97
French League
  championship 37–8,
  42, 44, 45, 47–8, 70,
  80, 131, 140
French national squad 171,
  174
  1990 36–7
  1993 62–5, 68–9
  1996 68, 162–4
  Under-21s 28

Garrincha 86
Gascoigne, Paul 28
Germany 165
GIGN force 38–9
Gillespie, Keith 120, 149,
  169
Ginola, Andrea (son of DG)
  15, 16, 68, 108, 109,
  111
  birth 77–8
Ginola, Carla (daughter of
  DG) 78, 114
Ginola, Coraline (wife of
  DG) 42, 43, 58, 62,
  65, 66, 148
  character 73, 74–6
  meets DG 76
  marries DG 77
  childbirth 77–8

  in Newcastle 107–8
Ginola, David
  character 9–10, 19,
  67–8, 73–5, 85–6,
  114, 127–8,
  168–9
  physique 20, 23, 37
  childhood 6–11, 13–22
  football apprenticeship
  18–23
  with Toulon club 23,
  25–30
  Matra Racing 30, 31–5
  Brest 35–9
  military service 32
  French national team
  36–7, 62–5, 68–9
  Paris Saint-Germain 33,
  41–4, 46–50, 51–2,
  65–6, 69–70, 79–87,
  89
  media exposure 52–9
  modelling 57–8
  marriage and children
  73–8
  with Newcastle United 1,
  2, 3, 58, 90, 91–8,
  99–105, 107–14,
  117–31, 133–43,
  145–58, 162, 166–9,
  172–4
  banned 126–30, 146–7,
  168
  transfer speculation
  170–72

in France, *1996* 159–64, 166–7
Ginola, Myrielle (mother of DG) 6, 13–14, 15, 16, 65, 66, 68
Ginola, René (father of DG) 5–6, 7–11, 13, 18–19, 23, 29, 43, 65, 66, 68
Ginola, Sebastian (brother of DG) 9–10
Giresse, Alain 27
Godallier, Olivier 55
golf 102
Graham, George 69
Grand Prix 161–2
Guerin, Vincent 49
Gullit, Ruud 92, 123

Hagi, Gheorghe 49
Hall, Sir John 92, 93, 96, 97, 123
Head of the Year award 162
Hearts 104
Heysel 66
Hillsborough 66
Hoddle, Glenn 151
Holland 49
Houllier, Gérard 63, 64–5, 66, 68, 69

Inter Milan 89, 90–1
Israel 63

Jacquet, Aimé 68, 162, 164

James, David 3
Jones, Rob 148
Jordan, Michael 84
Jorge, Artur
at Matra Racing 29–30, 33, 34, 110
with PSG 46, 65, 79–80, 110
Juventus 48

Keegan, Kevin 67
character 95, 154
hair 162
plays for Liverpool 17, 95
manager, Newcastle United 82, 91, 93, 95, 98, 102–3, 105, 108–10, 126, 135, 138, 139, 145, 146, 149, 150, 153–4, 155, 156, 169
Koeman, Ronald 49
Kombouaré, Antoine 48, 84–5
Kostadinov, Emil 63

Laccer, Francis 47–8
Lama, Bernard 35, 36, 84–5
languages 99–100
Le Guen, Paul 82
League championship, *1995–6* 134, 139–40, 156, 166–7
League Cup 137, 143

Lee, Rob 98
Leeds United 146, 148, 150
Legorju, Phillipe 38
Liverpool club 98, 148
   1977 17, 95
   1996 v. Newcastle United
     1, 2, 3, 136–8

Macari, Lou 124
McDermott, Terry 67,
     91, 92, 95, 126,
     155
managers 154
Manchester City 133
Manchester United 98, 123,
     130, 131
   manager 145
   and Newcastle United
     133–5, 136
     1996 138, 140, 142, 149,
     150, 151, 156, 166,
     167
   v. Nottingham Forest
     146
Maradona, Diego 37
Mardi Gras 128–9
Marley, Bob 84
Marseille club (Olympique;
     OM) 45–6, 52, 119
   interest in DG 38, 41–2
   rivalry with PSG 42–4
   bribery scandal 44–5
   1990 35
   1995 86
Martigues, nr. Marseille 43

Martins, Correntin 35
Matra Racing (Racing
     Paris) 29–30, 31–5
media exposure 52–9
Metz 27
Middlesbrough 119, 131
military service 32
modelling 56, 57–8
Monaco 151, 161–2
Montpellier 35
music 140–41

Napoli 173
Newcastle 99–100, 101,
     107–13
   DG's house burgled 53,
     171
Newcastle United
   management 96–8,
     109–10
   signs DG 58, 90, 91–4
   training camp 95–6
   DG meets team 95
   DG's first season with
     103–5, 117–31,
     133–43, 145–58, 165,
     166–9
   v. Arsenal 123, 124–6,
     128, 147
   v. Liverpool 1, 2, 3,
     136–8
   v. Manchester United
     133–5
   v. QPR 141–2
   v. Tottenham 150–51

end-of-season holiday 159
refuses offers for DG 170–72
DG's 2nd season 172–4
Nice
club 27–8
centre de formation 18–23, 25
v. Toulon 27
Mardi Gras 128–9
Nottingham Forest 146, 147, 149
Ntamack, Emile 58
nuclear tests 111

Olympique Marseille *see* Marseille club
Only Fools and Horses (tv programme) 105

Papin, Jean-Pierre 52, 63
Paris 32, 42, 108, 111, 171
DG in with Coraline 77
DG's son born in 77–8
Matra Racing club 29–30, 31–5, 36, 46, 81
modelling in 57–8
Saint-Germain club (PSG) 3, 46–50, 51–2, 62, 70, 87, 92, 131, 139, 167, 169, 173
DG joins 41–4

captaincy 82–3
managed by Fernandez 33, 79–86
managed by Jorge 46, 79–80
refuses to sell DG 69–70
DG leaves 86–7, 89
rivalry with Marseille 42–4
shirts 44
at Toulouse, *1993* 65–6
Pelé 37
penalty shoot-outs 164–5
Platini, Michel 17, 36–7, 103
Player of the Month 120
Player of the Year 70
Premier League 156, 157; *see also* League championships
prices for players 97–8

Queens Park Rangers (QPR) 141–2, 143, 152

Rai 110
Real Madrid 48
referees 125–8, 146–7, 165–6
Ricardo 86
Robert, Gaby 23, 25–6
Rocastle, David 28–9
Rocheteau, Dominique 55

Sedoc, Franklin 91
Selhurst Park 127
Senna, Ayrton 161
Sergi 49
sharks 61–2
Shearer, Alan 172
Sheffield Wednesday
      118–19
skiing 15, 18, 121
smoking 112
snow 122
Souss, Ibrahim 38
Spartak Moscow 49, 83
St Etienne club 14
   1977 17, 95
St Maxime, France 44
   DG's childhood in 2–3,
      6–11, 13–19, 21, 76
   DG's house in 56–7
   DG in, *1996* 159–61,
      162–3, 166
St Raphaël team 17
St Tropez, France 2, 6–7,
   14, 109
Stade Gerard Rossi 6, 15
star system 52–9
Stoichkov, Hristo 49

Tapie, Bernard 44
Thomas, Michael 28–9
Tigana, Jean 27

Tottenham Hotspur 150–51
Toulon club 23, 25–30,
      33–4, 69, 76
Toulouse 65
Touré, José 7
training 95–6, 102–3, 129
Tusseau, Thierry 27

UEFA 44
   Cup, *1993* 48

Valdo 48
Valenciennes 44

Waddle, Chris 119
Watson, Steve 125, 153
Weah, George 48, 49, 120,
      169
West Ham United 130, 135,
      136
Williams, Frank 161
Winterburn, Nigel 124, 125
women, English and
      French 113
World Cup
   1970 86
   1974 49
   1994 62–5, 71
   1998 171, 174

Yvinec, François 38